MW01243109

Boo! Can You See Us?

Faeven Realm Book One

Desy Smith

CONTENTS

This is a work of fiction. Names, characters, places, and incidents are either the product of the author's imagination or used fictitiously, and any resemblance to actual persons, living or dead, business establishments, events or locales is entirely coincidental.

Boo! Can You See Us? Faeven Realm Book One

Copyright 2021 Desy Smith

ALL RIGHTS RESERVED. This contains material protected under International and Federal Copyright Laws and Treaties. Any unauthorized reprint or use of this material is prohibited. No part of this book may be reproduced or transmitted in any form or by any means, electronic or mechanical, including photocopying, recording, or by any information storage and retrieval system without express written permission from the author/publisher.

PROLOGUE

OCTOBER 1984

The once-gray sky booms as a round of thunder hits it. I quicken my pace, inhaling the nauseating rose scent the rain left behind. Elf children dance in the rainbow puddles, oblivious to the fireflies. Finally, I spot the red and green twinkling lights and hurry, praying to the Goddess this is the right house, and she's home. I would never show up uninvited, but desperate times mean no decorum.

I knock on the silver, translucent door as lightning brightens the chocolate sky, revealing streaks of silver.

"Mommy!" A tiny hand tightly squeezes my bigger one. "I'm scared."

I look down at my adorable son, Leonardo. His lips are stained red from the magical sucker he was sucking on earlier. I called myself sneaking out, but Leonardo caught me red-handed, so here we are. Bending into a squat, I wince as a sharp pain travels up my back. Leonardo, the observant child he is, notices, and his eyes widen.

"Mommy?"

"Leo," I say with a placid smile. "Have I told you the story about the rain and the skilled warrior named Leonardo?"

"Hey, that's my name," Leo says and returns my smile. "Is this story about me?"

"Maybe," I reply, kissing his nose. "When we get home, I'll tell you the story."

His little lips poke out. "Okay."

I notice his hat is not on top of his head. Instead, he has it clutched in his left hand.

"Leo..." He looks up at me, his enormous eyes, similar to my own, blinking. "Remember, you promised if you came with Mommy, the hat stays on."

He huffs. "Okay, Mommy."

Leo quickly puts it back on and grabs my hand again. Using the wall as leverage, I rise, ignoring the pain in my back. I knock again, louder than before. Where are you, Sweetie?

"Coming," a childlike voice answers as a mature one chastises it.

"Do not answer that door, Faith!"

Giggling fills the house, followed by the sound of footsteps. The door opens and a little Elf girl around Leo's age appears before Sweetie pushes her out of the way. "Wait until Daddy hears about this," Sweetie tells Faith, shaking her head.

"Mommy's mean!" Faith replies.

I hear more footsteps and another door being slammed shut. Sweetie turns her attention back to me and takes a slow step back as her pointed ears twitch.

"I'm sorry, I think you have the wrong..." She trails off as I unwrap the scarf from around my face. "My Queen!"

She gasps and curtsies, but I bring a finger to my lips and re-wrap the scarf.

"What are you doing here, My Queen?" Sweetie whispers as she motions for me to come in.

The smell of bread and Elf stew fills my nose as I step inside the small cottage, pulling Leo close behind. My stomach growls, and I'm reminded it's past my suppertime.

"You wanna play with me?" Faith asks, looking in Leo's direction.

She's sitting on the stairs, smiling from ear to ear. Leo looks to me, his eyes wide with excitement.

"Go ahead, but keep the hat on," I tell him.

"Let's play ghost soldiers!" Leo exclaims and runs after her.

"I don't know how to play that," Faith replies with a giggle.

I turn back to Sweetie. "I need an emergency reading." Sweetie opens her mouth to protest, but I cut her off before she has the chance. "I will pay you double!"

"It's not about the money, My Queen." Sweetie swallows hard and takes a step closer to me. "I love giving you readings, but your husband," she glances around the room as if my husband is going to pop out any moment, "the king has forbidden me from giving you any additional readings."

"The king..." I pause as my gaze travels around the room, making sure no ghosts are present. "It is because of him that I've come to you."

I unbutton my trench coat and open it to show her my very pregnant belly.

"Oh, Fairy Goddess..." Sweetie covers her mouth and takes a step back. "I should have warned you."

At least, I believe that's what she's said, but it came out muffled so I can't be sure. I close my trench coat, buttoning it quickly, and ask, "Why, what have you seen?"

She removes her hand from her mouth. "Death."

Sweetie turns quickly and motions for me to follow.

Death? That wasn't the word I expected her to say. Is that my baby's fate, to die?

"My Queen," Sweetie says softly, now standing at an open door, urging me forward with a wave of her hand. Reluctantly, I move my feet.

I started getting readings years ago when it was a trend. Back then, I was being read by an older lady. She was close to my age, four or five hundred years old. One day, I came to her shop, and Sweetie informed me she no longer worked there. I allowed Sweetie to read me and thought nothing would come from it, as nothing ever had from the other lady. But Sweetie was different. All of her predictions —both the good and bad—came true. She is an oracle, and though it is not common in our realm, they do exist.

The smell of Palo Santo hits me hard, instantly putting me at ease. A table with various crystals, small tea light candles, and sage arranged in a geometric pattern sits in the middle of the room, flanked by two chairs. She gestures to one before walking around the table to hers.

"Have a seat."

I lower myself into the chair, ignoring the tight pain in my belly, and ask, "What do you need me to do?"

"I need your hands," she says.

Each time she's foretold my future, she's done it a different way. One time was with tarot cards, another time a pendulum, a time before that with tea leaves. I never question her methods. Whatever works, works.

"Both hands?"

"Yes," Sweetie replies as she extends her arms, palms up.

Carefully, I place my hands on top of her warm ones. A bead of sweat slides down my cheek and between my breasts. There's no turning back now.

"The child you carry," her eyes close, "will be different."

Yes, I gathered as much. I lean in, worried about the baby's death.

"She's a girl."

I gasp. I've always wanted a girl, a mini-me.

Without warning, the candles blow out and the open door slams closed, startling me. Quickly, I take my eyes off of Sweetie and examine the room again for ghosts. They are dramatic creatures. When I find none, I look back to Sweetie, whose eyes are wide open and white—no pupil, just white. No matter how many times she's done this, seeing her this way is extremely unnerving.

"She will be powerful," Sweetie continues, "even more powerful than the king's grandmother. Her powers will rival your husband's, and he will kill her for it."

No! He would never... Not his own child.

I snatch my hands from hers and stand. The sudden movement makes my head spin and the snack I ate earlier threatens to make a reappearance. Steadying myself, I grab the table.

"Only your daughter and her mate stand a chance against your husband's wrath."

Mate? Why is Sweetie using that term and not our term, soulie?

"Her mate will protect her at all costs, as she will protect him."

The baby kicks from inside me as a few stray tears slide down my cheek. He wouldn't kill her, right? This is his child—his flesh and blood.

"How do I stop this?" I ask, reaching for her hands again. "Sweetie, please tell me how to stop this."

"Kill him."

No...

"It is the only way."

I can't, he's my soulie.

"Kill him before he kills your daughter!"

CHAPTER 1

LUNA

A warm arm snakes around my waist, pulling me close to a hard body with a very profound erection.

"I know you're not asleep." How would he know that when he's been gone most of the evening? "Your maid informed me you were angrily pacing the bedroom, threatening to throw my belongings off the balcony." He chuckles deeply.

Dramatically sighing, I wiggle from his embrace and straddle him. The moonlight streaming through the open curtains allows me to see the knowing smirk on his face. He thinks we're about to make love and all will be forgiven, but not this time. His days of manipulating me are over.

"You promised you would go to the gala with me." He slowly lifts my silk negligee over my hips, exposing my bare ass. "We had a deal."

"My love, I promise you, it was not intentional."

One hand grips my ass while the other pulls down a silk strap.

"The Sups think I'm single." Gently, he bites my left nipple through my gown. I roll my eyes in ecstasy as a warmth and wetness settle between my legs. No, I cannot let him distract me. "They think you've abandoned me.

"Find me," he says, removing my negligee in one swift movement. "Luna, come find me," he says again, rising and gently laying me on my back. "Luna, *find* me!"

PRESENT, 2010

The honking of a horn brings me out of my thoughts, and I glance in my rearview mirror and floor it.

I've been having dreams like this, of this man and our incredible sex life since I turned eighteen... seven years ago. But about a year ago, the dreams slightly changed. Now, instead of mind-blowing sex, he demands I find him.

From my perception, we'd make a great couple, even though he stands me up more times than I like to admit. He's still a great man. But I know I'm not the best woman for him. I have a problem. And no, I'm not talking about acne or even my propensity to say random stuff when I find myself nervous. It's far worse than that.

Stomping on my brakes as the light suddenly turns red, I tell myself to focus. *He doesn't exist,* I say for the millionth time. *Stop pondering your dream and focus.* My attention wanders to the water fountain, where I notice a woman with blemish-free, dark mahogany skin about my age but skinnier. Way skinnier.

Angrily, she's yelling and gesturing at the lingering people hanging by the waterfall. My windows are up so I can't hear what she says exactly, but I know what she wants. Suddenly, as if sensing my presence, she turns and locks eyes with me. Crap. Her eyes widen as a knowing smile overtakes her face. I groan as she vanishes.

Yes, she's dead, and if you haven't figured it out by now, I can see ghosts.

The water show stops and slowly descends, leaving dark, black smoke in its wake. It rises, imitating the water show before disintegrating into thin air. I've never seen that before.

A loud pop echoes in my car as the ghost that was dancing in the fountain reappears in the passenger seat next to me. The sound of another horn makes me jump, and I quickly take my foot off the brake and stomp on the gas, accelerating through the light.

"Oh, my... Fairy Goddess, you *can* see me!" she exclaims.

I continue driving, glancing in my rearview mirror at the fountain, wondering if the black smoke will appear again. But it doesn't. What *was* that smoke?

"Hello! I know you hear me."

Ghosts are toddlers; they do what they want, when they want, and because of them, I will never look for the sexy man in my dreams.

"Hello!" she screams.

"Yes, I can hear you. Can you stop screaming?" I reply with a sigh. She crosses her arms over her insanely large bust and smirks. "What do you want?"

"I want to figure out how I became... Well, you know..." She trails off. I don't have to look at her to know she's gesturing to herself. "How can you see me?"

"Call it a gift," I tell her. And then, to myself, I whisper, "Or a curse."

I turn and release an involuntary scream and accidentally jerk the steering wheel as I find myself nose to nose with her. For some odd reason, ghosts can touch me and I them. I can't explain it, but when they're around me, they are very much alive.

"Why are you so close to me?!" I yell.

She lets out a huff and plops back in her seat. "I wanted to smell you."

Here's your first lesson in Ghost 101: #1—Many people assume your senses disappear when you die, but that's not completely accurate. Ghosts have four of the five senses: sight, smell, sound, and touch.

I finally pull into my apartment complex, able to give her my undivided attention.

13

"Name; what is it?" I ask.

"Za'Riyah," she instantly replies, letting me know she's just recently died.

Ghost 101: #2—It's not uncommon for a ghost to not remember its name. Depending on how long ago they died, they forget who they are, how they died, and other important details about their life. Of course, each ghost is different.

"Okay, Riyah." I cut off the Za because I'm petty and she deserves it for causing me to swerve and nearly wreck my car.

"No, Za'Riyah," she replies, slowly enunciating her name.

"Gotcha, Riyah."

She mumbles something unintelligible under her breath.

"Riyah, why were you sniffing me?" I ask, my curiosity getting the better of me.

"To see if you're Human, silly, and you're definitely not."

I hold up my hand. She can't be serious. "What? You say 'Human' as if there's a possibility there are some other species when there's not."

"What reason would I have to lie?" She glares, twirling a stray curl around her finger. "Is it really so hard to believe me when Angels are living in your realm, your Earth?"

She has a point there.

"Those are Angels," I reply. Angels' sole purpose is to protect Humans. "Angels are harmless."

"They built your Earth on the blood of their victims."

Wow. "That's dark."

"Yes, but it's the truth." She rolls her eyes. "Anyway, you are not Human."

"And you're an Angel?" I ask because she doesn't resemble one.

"Ew, no!"

"Well, how would you know I'm not Human?"

"Because I'm not Human either."

Sure she's not. Maybe I was wrong about how long she's been dead because she's clearly forgotten she once was Human.

"Listen, I don't know if you serious or not, but if you're joking, I won't—"

Wings—dainty, beautiful butterfly wings—emerge from her back.

Oh, my God. The wings have to be eight to ten inches long, four to five inches wide, and absolutely gorgeous. They're the color of a ripe eggplant, with a plum lining and a dash of black glitter. On television, Fairy wings—since that's what I assume she is—are bright, vibrant colors like blue, red, or pink with silver glitter. Yet here she is, the complete opposite of the so-called norm.

"Eggplants. You have eggplants on your back," my mouth spews, repeating what I've said inside my mind. I shake my head. This is what I meant when I said I blurt random stuff out when I'm nervous or scared, and right now, I'm both.

"What?" Riyah questions, and begins messing with that loose curl again.

"I... Um, nothing."

"I know you're freaking out."

"You'd freak out too if you just realized—"

"I wouldn't," she replies, quickly cutting me off.

"You would so!"

She shakes her head. "Accept it and move on."

"But—"

"Move *on*."

I don't want to admit this, but she's right. Me losing my shit over this latest discovery won't change the fact she's not Human. Also, her being whatever she is shouldn't be all that surprising since I can talk to ghosts. I take a deep breath.

"So what are you?"

I reach out a hand to touch her wings, but she swats it away. Just as quickly as the wings appeared, they vanish.

"We only allow our smooch—boyfriend or girlfriend in Human lingo—to touch our wings."

I nod my understanding. "Riyah, what are you?" I ask again.

"Isn't it obvious?" Yes, it is, but I need to hear her say it.

After a long, dramatic pause, she replies, "I'm a Fairy."

"Where are you from? Where do you live?"

She chuckles. "Well, non-Human girl, once again, I'm a Fairy." I open my mouth to repeat my previous questions, but she holds up a finger. "I'm not done speaking yet."

Riyah clears her throat, and I refrain from sighing. I can tell her personality is over the top, and I say a prayer that I don't have to put up with her for much longer.

"We live in another realm." Realms, I've heard that term before. "Yes, non-Human girl, there are six realms."

The Angels! That's who spoke about the realms. They're always mentioning the "Six Realms." A million questions run through my mind, but one stands at the forefront.

"You said I'm not Human. Do you know what I am?"

She runs her fingers through her hair and opens her mouth, but suddenly, her animated eyes become vacant.

"You scared me." She giggles, and her hand gently hits the dashboard. "I hope my brother didn't see you come in."

There's a long stretch of silence before she screams once as her body doubles over. With shaking hands, she reaches for her abdomen, and raises one hand, looking at it intensely before her eyes roll to the back of her head and she falls backward, her head hitting the window behind her.

Ghost 101: #3—All ghosts have moments where they relive their deaths. Some relive it in its entirety. Others only relive bits and pieces. It depends on the ghost, and the moment comes when it wants to come. There's no controlling it.

Riyah opens her eyes, mindlessly staring ahead before she blinks once and pops up, smiling again. "What were we talking about?"

Ghost 101: #4—After ghosts re-experience their death, they never remember they've relived it. I've learned that bringing it up does more harm than good, so I pretend it didn't happen.

"I asked you if you know what I am?"

"It's on the tip of my tongue and yet..." She messes with that curl again. "I don't remember." Well, thanks for nothing. "But we can remedy that." I know where this is going. "Come to my realm, help me find my killer, and we will figure it out together."

"I don't know about that."

Za'Riyah invades my personal space once again, gripping my shoulders tightly. I keep my face nonchalant, not wanting her to know she's hurting me. I've learned to never give ghosts the upper hand.

"If you don't help me, I will hunt you for the rest of your pathetic non-Human life," she threatens as her grip tightens. "I will make your life miserable."

I roughly remove her hands from my shoulders. "You can try."

Feeling done with the conversation, I get out of the car and leave her inside. As soon as I slam the door, I hear the popping sound. I turn, and she's directly in front of me.

"Sorry, sorry, sorry," she whines loudly and dramatically. I roll my eyes. "I'm serious! I realize now that threatening isn't how I should handle this, even though it's second nature for my kind."

Second nature? What does she mean by that? Who uses threats to make someone do something? Do I want to go to that world?

"Uh-huh."

She blows that loose curl out of her face. "Listen, I have no clue what it's like to be... Human," she snorts on the word, "however, you are not meant for this realm, and deep down, you know it." She grips my face with both hands. Why is she so touchy-feely? "You belong with your kind."

I'm adopted, and I love Mom, Dad, my two sisters, and two brothers. I couldn't ask for a better family. But none of them, of course, can see ghosts, except my biological brother Leo, who I met five years ago and is seldom around. I'd be lying if I said I wasn't curious about my birth family and the ghost powers I'm sure I inherited from them.

"But if you enjoy this pathetic realm and the—"

"I'm in."

I know I need to do this. If I don't like what I see or who they are, I can always come back, right? Za'Riyah squeals and begins jumping up and down, forcing me to jump up and down with her.

"Great! Are you up for a brief field trip tonight?"

CHAPTER 2

CAIRO

"Did you hear me, Your Excellency?"

My attention turns to King Max, the Elf King and representative for his Sups. I nod once, yet my mind is elsewhere, per usual of late. I take in the sitting room—my Dragon's favorite sitting room, mind you. Three different sheer shades of brown cover the eleven windows, each forty-eight inches in width. The sun peeks from the many clouds that conceal my palace and shines through the fabric, making the golden tile under my feet sparkle.

On the east wall, a grand translucent piano with gold trimming is nestled between four large brown bookshelves, books I've read four times over. On the west wall, a large portrait of my Dragon is painted in his likeness, surrounded by the ten Dragons of the only other Dragon family here in Faeven.

In front of me, on the north wall, sits an insanely large wet bar with gold trimming. It is filled with all the popular drinks in Faeven; from Witches' brew to Fairy wine, I have it all. Finally, the south wall, where the current queen and kings and I sit are ten separate Lazy Boy silk brown chairs, facing each other in a circle of sorts.

I have so much, and I should be grateful, but it's not enough. I do not want more, but I want something else... and yet, I can't articulate what it is.

"I think not. His mind is elsewhere, as it always is," Queen Vickie, the light Fairy mutters under her breath, knowing I'll hear her.

"It would be wise for you to remember your place, Vickie," King Stef, the dark Fairy, venomously spits as he suddenly stands to his feet and paces the room.

King Max turns his attention to him. "You shouldn't have come, Stephen. Your family and the queen need you now. We can—"

"You can *what?*" Stef advances toward him, an angry scowl on his face. "You can't do this without me." He bangs his chest. "I am the brains in this operation of yours."

So he would think.

"If only in your dreams, you are," Queen Vickie whispers.

King Max's ears twitch, having heard her. He swallows but doesn't comment.

"Did you say something?" King Stef questions, eyes on Vickie as he moves toward her.

"Enough of this," I reply in my no-nonsense voice, leaving no room for argument.

Queen Vickie stares intensely at her nails as if she hasn't purposely riled Stef, who mutters something under his breath about missing his opportunity to kill her a century ago. He then moves to the wet bar to fix himself a drink, a Witches' brew, minus the ice.

My Dragon, who was sleeping peacefully, awakens and snorts; irritated Stef is consuming our libations yet again.

"King Stephen, if I haven't expressed my condolences, please let me do so now." He lifts his glass toward me in acknowledgment and then stares into it. "I assure you I will find who's responsible for your daughter's death, and I will serve justice."

My Dragon nods, agreeing.

20

Stef looks up from his glass to gaze out of the window with tear-filled eyes. "I want him to suffer. I want him to *suffer.*"

Max was correct in his earlier statement. He should be home, mourning with his family. However, even with my title, I cannot tell someone how to grieve. My Dragon snorts, letting me know he disagrees. If it were up to him, I'd have a say-so about everything in the royal's day-to-day life. Good thing the decision isn't his, and, much to his annoyance, he knows it.

"Shall we get to the bottom of why we're here, Your Excellency?" Queen Vickie looks at me, and I nod. "He must be stopped."

"I agree," King Max says, his fist hitting his palm.

"I do as well," King Stef says while pouring himself a second drink before turning his attention back to us. "He came to my home and, in front of my wife, offered to summon my daughters' spirit!" Stef swallows the contents in one gulp.

"He did no such thing!" Queen Vickie says, her mouth gaped and a hand over her chest.

Stef uses his long sleeve to wipe his mouth and replies, "He claimed it was so we could say our last goodbyes."

King Max comments, "He knows as well as all the other royals that it's against our law to raise someone with royal blood from the dead. It disturbs the order of things."

He's right. Intentionally raising someone with royal blood, with that much power in their veins, never goes right. More times than none, their soul, the very essence of who they are, has left their body and ascended. What's left to occupy the deceased body is something dark and demonic, ready to wreak havoc in our realm.

"He has spirits working for him," Queen Vickie mumbles.

"We can't do anything about that," King Max says with a shrug. "It's like Elves working for me or light Fairies working for you, Vickie. The dead are essentially his to command."

"That is not what I speak of..."

"Then be clear with your words, Vickie. We have not the time to—"

21

"Rumor has it," Vickie lowers her voice, "instead of performing last rites to send the spirits on their way, he keeps them in his employ. Some as servants, others as prisoners."

This is news to me. My Dragon lazily blinks, unbothered by the news, and I don't know if that's a good or bad thing.

"And you know this to be true *how*?" King Max asks.

"His servant told my servant," Vickie answers matter-of-factly.

"The world must be ending if you're choosing to engage in conversation with your employees," Max says with a roll of his eyes.

"I'll have you know that I speak to everyone from the top to the bottom."

"I cannot issue a warning without concrete evidence, Queen Victoria, nor can I speak to King Alastair because his maid told your maid something."

"He offered to raise his deceased daughter from the dead," Vickie gestures toward Stef, "and I believe that is treason."

"No, it is not. It's just the words of a man who is sympathetic to a grieving king and queen about their daughter."

My Dragon chuckles, knowing that's a lie.

"Hearsay, all hearsay!" King Stef shouts, forcing our attention on him. He's pouring himself drink number three.

Yes, he's right, it is hearsay.

Vickie says, "It is not hearsay. He has been doing this for decades, and we have done nothing. Cowardice all of us, all of *you*."

The comment is generalized, but Vickie is looking at only me.

Your response. I direct the thought to my Dragon. He slowly blinks before closing his eyes.

"You can't be serious, Cairo," Max comments. "He has no sympathy for what Stef is going through, and he offered to do something he had no right to offer. It is a rule for a reason, which he agreed to when he became the Sovereign of the Necromancer community."

The door bursts open, and in walks King Alastair himself.

Suddenly, Vickie and Max stand to their feet while Stef pours himself drink number four.

"Oh, no. Please do not stand on my account," King Alastair says and struts toward Stef.

"Leave him be!" Vickie yells as Max shouts, "You have no right here!"

"*You* have no right to tell *me* what to do here, Queen Victoria. This is Our Excellency's castle in the sky, not yours."

He winks at me. Queen Victoria opens her mouth, but I hold up my hand and she shuts it with a huff before plopping back into her seat, legs crossed, glaring at the back of King Alastair's head.

Alastair says, "King Maximillian, you speak as if I'm not a ruler here in Faeven when we both know that's not true." Max blinks slowly. "Now to address the service I offered to King Stephen—"

"Service my ass," Vickie whispers, looking at me. Alastair pats Stephen's back a couple of times. "I was only offering my assistance. None of *you* can contact the dead."

Stephen shakes Alastair's hand off his back, places the glass on the wet bar, grabs the decanter, which is still half-full, and walks out the open door. "

Alastair looks at us. "Touchy, isn't he?"

"You bastard!" Queen Vickie yells, surprising me. "His daughter just died."

"Why offer to raise his daughter when you know it is against our laws?" Max questions.

I too wonder the reason behind this. My Dragon opens his eyes, curious as well.

"He mistook my words; I did not mean raise in the undead-zombie sense." He waves his hand around. "What I was suggesting is a simple commune with her spirit, which I'm sure has crossed over by now." He claps. "Harmless."

My Dragon snorts, labeling him a liar.

"That's a lie if I ever heard one," Max whispers under his breath.

Vickie questions, "Why are you here?"

"Why are you all having a meeting without me, without the rest of us?"

"Why are you such—"

"Such a what, Queen Victoria?"

I ask, "Need I remind you, you came to my castle uninvited?"

My Dragon nods his head, agreeing.

King Alastair bows. "My apologies, My Excellency." He dramatically sighs and I wonder where he's going with this...

"There is no secret meeting." The lie rolls off my tongue easily. "I only possess the patience to meet with these three at the moment." Another lie. "I will meet with the rest of you in a few days."

"Yes, Your Excellency. I suppose watching us and making sure we behave keeps you rather... busy," King Alastair replies with heavy sarcasm. My Dragon blows smoke, upset by Alastair's tone. "But I am rather bored," King Alastair adds.

"Whose fault is that?" I question.

"No disrespect, but yours, My Excellency, since I'm not allowed to leave this realm."

"Ahh, yes." I smile. "Your punishment; what was it? A decade?"

Alastair sneers. "Two."

"Yes, which you've only served eighteen years of."

"Will I be required to serve the other two?"

"Do you wish to air your grievance about your punishment in front of others?"

He glares at me before a smile appears. "Of course not, Your Excellency. Shall I schedule an appointment?"

"Yes. I believe you should."

WINDOW OPEN, blinds drawn up, I lean against the wall and listen to the nightlife of the city in the Human realm. My Dragon snorts. He despises the putrid odor of Human sweat, feces, and pollution from the realm known as Dallas. Due to the Angels openly announcing their presence, the Human world knows of our kind.

My Dragon huffs, calling me out on my lie.

Correction—the Humans are only *aware* of Angels; they're still in the dark about the other realms and other Sups, including myself. However, the Angels believe themselves to be superior to the other Sups and claimed Earth as their home realm. My Dragon growls, hating that those pretty creatures thought they could match his strength.

The Angels allowed us, representatives from the other realms, an office of our choosing in "their" realm. I chose here, Dallas, as I was drawn to this place. That was nearly a decade ago, and whatever or whoever drew me here has yet to make an appearance inside the small, stuffy office.

Pam, my hired personal assistant, comes in without bothering to knock. She takes one look at the open window and shakes her head.

"You know how I feel about smelling this Dallas. It makes me ill."

She stomps over to the window, shuts it, and lowers the blinds. I sit behind my desk and dial my voicemail. Zero messages. No surprise there.

"You needed something?" I ask her, noticing she's still present.

Pam takes a seat. "It is such unfortunate news about the murder of Za'Riyah..."

"Yes," I reply.

Murders happen in Faeven but not often. For a royal to be murdered is unheard of.

"Can I be frank?" Pam questions, and my Dragon rolls his eyes. When is she not frank?

"You may."

"My coven and I are all scared shitless. If a royal isn't safe, us commoners stand no chance." I flinch at the word "commoners." She knows how I feel about the term. "Do you have any leads on who killed her?"

"No, none yet," I reply, although I do believe King Alastair is somehow involved. But I have no proof.

"You don't think..." She lowers her voice, even though it's only us two on the floor. "You don't think another royal did this?"

I do.

"Do not make such accusations, Pam," I reply, shutting down the true statement.

She exhales in relief. "Yes," she laughs, "silly me."

Pam rises from her seat, smiling and no longer worried. I truly wish what I said was true. Things are changing in Faeven and not for the better.

CHAPTER 3

LUNA

I frown up at the four-story police station, wondering why I agreed to our little "field trip." I'd rather be home, cuddled up with my fuzzy blanket, sipping spiked hot cocoa. Before I forget, I send a quick text to my birth brother, Leo, filling him in about Za'Riyah and the black shadow in the water fountain. Then I turn my attention in her direction.

"Riyah?"

She's twirling that loose curl around her pointer finger. "Yes?" she says, but her thoughts are elsewhere.

"Why are we at a cop station in the middle of the night?"

She slaps her forehead with her palm and dramatically exhales. "I keep forgetting; you think you're Human, so you don't know."

"Well...?" I put my hands on my hips, waiting for some sort of explanation.

Ignoring me, she smiles and disappears before reappearing behind the front door of the police station. Here we go.

The inside of this station differs from the others I've visited when helping ghosts. An elevator greets us as soon as we walk in the front entrance, followed by a large reception desk where an officer sits, answering phones. Behind it are smaller desks, the majority of them empty, with a large office against the back wall. Riyah stops directly in front of the elevator and turns to face me. I wait for the cop sitting at the reception desk to greet me, but he never does.

"Why haven't they acknowledged me?" I ask out loud.

"Silly, they can't see you," she giggles, "and this proves once more that you aren't Human."

Her statement makes little sense. "I'm pretty sure I've been here before and they acknowledged me."

"Yeah, probably because you walked to the reception desk and spoke to whoever was sitting there, right?"

"Well... yes."

"A Witch—"

"There are Witches in your world, too?"

"Accept it and move on," Riyah demands. "Say it!"

"But you said nothing—"

"Accept it and move *on*," Riyah says again, more sternly than before. "Now say it."

"I'm accepting it and moving on," I repeat with a glare.

"Great!" She claps her hands. "Yes, a Witch spelled the police building so that anyone Fae-related is undetected. Of course, the spell is void if you go up there and start a conversation." Okay, *that* makes sense. "Now, press the elevator button," she adds as she points to the "up" button.

I know you're wondering, after the many ghost movies you've seen courtesy of television: shouldn't she be able to push the button herself? Well, the answer is complicated.

Ghost 101: #5—Ghosts gain control over physical objects the longer they've been dead. Newer ghosts—the ones who've just passed away—can push buttons or knock things over, but it doesn't happen overnight. It requires practice. Ghosts that have been dead ten or more years can interfere with electricity and manipulate the climate in a particular room. Those who've been dead for thirty-plus years, otherwise known as "the headaches"—I suggest everyone steer clear—

can body-jump, meaning they can take over your body and dump you into their ghost one.

I can't help but shiver as I think back to that experience.

Riyah and I step inside the elevator, and a thought occurs to me.

"Won't they see the elevator door opening?"

"Yeah. They think the place haunted," she replies with a giggle. "They're talking about moving."

"It's not funny."

Take it from someone who knows. Being haunted or thinking you're haunted is not fun.

"Geesh, you're a serious one." She clears her throat. "Now place either hand on the elevator panel," I do as she says, "and repeat these words: 'The leaves in Faeven are always golden in the spring.'"

There goes that word again. "What the heck is a fav-on?"

"Faeven; it's pronounced fa-v-in," she responds.

"Same thing."

"No, it is not. The name is Faeven. It's the realm I'm from, and you must pronounce it correctly if you want this to work." She runs her fingers through her hair. "I would do it but, you know..."

She gestures to herself. Ghosts love reminding you of their current predicament.

"Fine, fine."

I clear my throat, remembering the pronunciation she used, and repeat it exactly. The elevator squeaks and the doors slam shut. Suddenly fearful, I take a step back. Glancing at the panel again, I see a fifth-floor option, highlighted in gold. When did that get there? I turn to Riyah, who's clapping her hands excitedly. What have I gotten myself into?

"Wh-where—" I stutter and swallow. "When did that fifth-floor button appear? Why did the doors slam shut like that? Are you taking me somewhere to kill me? I swear to God, if you try anything, I'll make it my life's mission to make sure you never cross over."

Mute, she smiles mischievously just as the elevator comes to an abrupt stop, squeaks once more, and, according to the panel, opens on the fifth floor.

"Floors one through four are for the Humans, but the fifth floor, and *only* the fifth floor, is ours. The Fae floor," she adds and steps out. "Follow me."

I peek my head out, noticing a dimly lit hall and a small pool of light where a bored middle-aged woman sits at a desk, reading. There's a door to the left of her, unmarked and closed, and another one to her right that reads "washroom," and that's it. This is the Faeven police department?

I don't know what I was expecting, but this is a total letdown, I think to myself as we make our way down the hallway.

"Ugh, a Witch," Riyah says, appearing next to me. "We may be here all night."

Do the Fairies in Faeven dislike all Witches, or is this just Riyah being her annoying self? I bet the latter.

Turning my attention to said Witch, I frown. I didn't expect a Witch to look so, um... Human. Her face is round, and her hair is cut into a stylish bob. Her face isn't green, nor does she have a large banana nose or warts as portrayed on TV.

"She doesn't look Witchy at all."

"I beg your pardon!" the Witch says.

Oops, I must have said that out loud. "It's just, you aren't green, and, well, you're not ugly," I blurt out.

She sighs. "Don't tell me you totally buy into that green-painted-face crap?"

"Painted?" I reply, genuinely confused.

"Yes, the green paint Humans wear on their faces for Halloween, when in reality, the green face was originally just a facial on spa day."

Where is she going with this? She sees the confusion plastered on my face and continues.

"Yeah, a spa facial. One of the dumbest of the dumb Humans somehow found his way into our realm. He stumbled into my family's coven and caught my eldest sister relaxing, wearing a green facial hydration spa mask."

"Seriously?"

"Please don't get her started or we'll be here all night," Riyah comments and exhales.

I still have so many questions. "What about the—"

The sound of someone clearing their throat turns my attention. I look at Riyah, who is exhaling again.

"Could you stop all the small talk and listen to me?" she whines.

"What?" I ask, and keep my attention on the Witch.

The Witch tilts her head and squints her eyes. "I didn't say anything."

Ignoring her, I wait for Riyah to continue.

"I need you to ask if any important Fairy corpses have been discovered in the Faeven database."

Ignoring the important comment, I ask the question. The Witch gives me a long look before she replies with a firm no.

"I'm sorry, but who are you?" the Witch questions.

Riyah waves her off, going from extremely annoying to very entitled. Who does she think she is?

"Ask her how she's so sure." She points to the desk. "I don't see any computers or anything."

She's right. Unlike the Human police station on the first floor, which was buzzing with life and technology, the Faeven police station seems to be here only as a front, as if the proper police station is behind one of the two closed doors.

"Are you sure?" I ask the Witch, curious as well.

"Are you talking to me now, or...?"

I sigh. "Yes, you."

"Yes, yes, I'm sure," she replies rather smugly. "I'm a Witch, as you very well know."

I don't mention that I learned Witches were real only a few minutes ago.

"Does being a Witch mean you suddenly know when someone

passes away?" I ask, unable to help myself. Does she receive a magical scroll each time someone dies or something?

"No, but they are nosey creatures. Nothing happens without them knowing," Riyah comments. "Oh! Describe me to her."

"How did you get up here, and what are you?"

Ignoring her, I continue. "The Fairy I'm talking about, she's close to my age, skinny, like super skinny, brown-mahogany complexion, and long, beautiful, unruly, curly hair—"

"Hey!" Riyah exclaims, but I continue.

"—that appears to be blue-black, a heart-shaped face, and wings." I have to make sure I mention the wings. "Oh, and her name is Riyah. Well, Za'Riyah."

The Witch's mouth drops open.

"I think you broke her," Riyah says, sounding genuinely shocked. I have to agree.

"Cairo!" the Witch screams.

When this Cairo doesn't appear, she continues shouting the name, louder and louder, like a raving lunatic. The closed, unlabeled door opens with such force that it bangs against the wall.

"Woman," a deep, masculine voice roars from inside the room. "I've told you time and time again not to repeatedly yell my name."

"Oh, did you?" the Witch questions, head cocked to the side with a flutter of her eyelashes.

"Pam, I do not—"

I gasp and mindlessly take a step back, bumping into Riyah.

"What's wrong?" Riyah asks, genuinely concerned.

It's *him*... The guy in my dreams, the one who told me to find him.

His skin is the color of bronzed gold. Think of gold in its purest form and darken it. He's tall, at least six foot six, but not lanky. He's nothing but muscle. I know because I've spent many dreams admiring his strong back, sculpted arms, and firm ass. His long jet-black hair is divided into plaits, with a thin red and gold ribbon neatly intertwined inside a few strands, gathered into a messy, high bun. If his skin, height, and hair didn't make him the most attractive man in the world, his face definitely does.

I swear when God was making the rest of us, he didn't give us much thought. He, however, took his time with this man. His face is diamond-jawed and accented with thick eyebrows that look as if they were just arched. His nose is a classic Roman shape, and his lips are full, fuller than mine, which is surprising because I have the lips all women dream of and pay for—so says my older sister, anyway. His round, gray eyes meet mine, and I can't look away.

He's real. The guy I've dreamed about since I turned eighteen is real, and he's here in front of me. An elbow in my side finally breaks the trance, and I turn to Riyah with a glare.

"I definitely wouldn't go there," Riyah says, and she disappears from my side before reappearing in front of me, blocking my view of Cairo. "We should go."

CHAPTER 4

CAIRO

One never knows how these moments will happen, and I never pictured meeting her this way. My mother would chastise me if she knew our first encounter was at a small, rather lackluster, outdated Sup police department in the Human world. I did not want this to be her first impression of me, and yet it is.

My Dragon, who was slumbering peacefully, awoke as soon as he smelled her vanilla-cinnamon aroma. Now he's pacing back and forth, urging me to go to her, yet I can't move. I can only stare, and—oh, Father—she is absolutely gorgeous and tall, five foot ten at least, which is wonderful. I love tall women.

She has a complexion that's a warm terracotta brown, and beautiful, round-slanted eyes, thinly arched eyebrows, and gorgeous brown eyes that appear hazel when the light hits them. Her nose is small, but those full lips are made for kissing, among other things. Beautiful black hair with brown highlights, cut short to her shoulders, accentuates her long neck.

My gaze travels down, taking in her full breasts that are hidden under a top that's missing a lot of fabric, but it reveals her toned belly.

Her pants appear to be a second skin, showing her hips—hips made for my rather large hands—and a nice-sized butt.

A poke in my bicep turns my attention to the only Sup comfortable enough to do it, Pam. She's currently looking back and forth between us both.

"Funny you both seem to have the same reaction to each other," Pam comments and snorts before a knowing grin spreads across her face. "Oh, my. I don't know why the Fairy Goddess bestowed this knowledge on little ole me, but I am most grateful."

My Dragon snorts, annoyed that Pam knows. I look back to my mate, whose name I realize I don't know.

"Did you, by chance, get her name?" I ask Pam, and she shakes her head.

"Hey! Girl who talks to herself!" Pam calls out to her. My mate, who was standing a few inches away from me only a few seconds ago, is now by the wall, arguing with someone neither Pam nor I can see. "What's your name?"

"Luna," she replies and turns around. "You never asked me for my name, which is why you didn't know," she says, directing the comment to the person we can't see.

"She's been doing this since she came in, Excellency," Pam informs me.

I could be wrong, but I think Luna is speaking to a ghost. My Dragon snarls, not appreciating me calling her by her birth-given name. I ignore him.

Lowering her voice, Luna says, "Again, you were the one who asked me to come here. Remember, Za'Riyah?" Her hands are on her hips.

My Dragon lifts his head, surprised that's who she's talking to, and he's hardly ever surprised.

Pam turns to me. "If you're wondering, yes. Yes, she said Za'Riyah." I nod. "The dark Fairy princess is currently talking to your mate."

It would appear so. Such a small world...

A sharp pain appears without warning inside my head and a masculine voice says, "Her power will rival his, and for this, he will kill her. Once she becomes a ghost, he will take over the world."

I blink, and the pain is gone as my Dragon lets me know that was my father's voice. Yes, it was, and it's been centuries since he's communicated with me in that fashion. What does it mean? My Dragon sighs, wanting me to focus on our mate, who's once again looking at me.

"Are you okay?" Luna hesitantly asks as she takes a step forward, appearing as if she's going to approach me, but pauses. Her arms move backward. "Okay, okay, we're going, Riyah," she announces, and looks over her shoulder.

My mate's eyes drift back to mine and again we stare at each other. My Dragon shakes his head, reminding me of my father's cryptic message, and it's then I realize what he means. Luna must be King Alastair's daughter, and if he gets his hands on her, he will kill her and use her ghost form to take over the world.

"Sorry for bothering you both," Luna says to Pam and me before turning around.

How didn't I notice it before? She is the spitting image of her mother, Queen Lilliana. I reach out, wanting to say something, but what? My Dragon stands to his full height and snorts, his way of telling me to take her, protect her, hide her away, and make her have our babies. Subtle he is not.

"There it is again," my mate comments, staring into the mirror in front of her.

Pam added it a year ago when she called herself starting a beauty channel that lasted two months. My Dragon snorts again, chastising me for allowing her to do it.

"Do you see it, Riyah?"

"Is this an only-she-can-see thing?" Pam questions.

"Yes," I answer, as I see nothing in the mirror

"Are you *sure* you haven't seen it before?" Luna is still looking to

Za'Riyah. "When you came to me from the fountain, it was there, too."

Pam and I, both curious, move toward her, but I still see nothing but her reflection.

"Describe what you're seeing," Pam says.

"Smoke. Moving smoke," Luna says as she stares into the mirror. "Calm down, Riyah. I'm sure it's..."

Her words fall away as her hand reaches toward the mirror and touches it. The mirror cracks down the middle and she gasps, her eyes widening.

"Fuck!" Luna exclaims and turns to Za'Riyah. "It's the shadow side. You'll need to go back to your place of death." She sighs and claps her hands in an annoyed fashion. "Well, I can't undo what I've just done." She nods. "I touched it, and now it's in our world."

I open my mouth to say something but pause when I see my breath. Did the temperature drop? I look around, noticing that the lighting in the room just got dimmer. My Dragon huffs, reminding me to stay alert.

"It's getting cold and dark in here," Pam comments as black smoke, which I can see now, seeps through the crack.

"Shield yourself," I tell Pam.

"What about you?" She looks up at me. "Will you be okay, Your Excellency?"

"Yes, now shield yourself."

I look back to my mate, who has both her hands raised, resting on Za'Riyah, I assume.

"Try again, Riyah," she continues. "If you can't do it yourself, I'll have to send you back and it's going to be painful." She's silent. "Are you sure?" More silence. "Okay." She takes a deep breath before exhaling. "Return."

"Ah!" Pam screams as the light hanging above our heads shatters.

Glass rains over us before plunging us into darkness. My Dragon takes over and my eyes half-shift.

"Are you okay?" I call out to my Luna. Her back is turned, and her arms are over her head, shielding herself.

"*I'm* quite fine," Pam responds.

I turn to glare at her as she stands with a knowing smile in her colorful bubble of protection. The darkness that was seeping from the mirror fills the entire room, and the feeling it invokes inside me gives me chills. What is this stuff?

I direct the question to my Dragon. He growls, letting me know these are spirits, evil spirits, the ones who refuse to cross over. My feet, having a mind of their own, move toward Luna. I notice there's glass lingering in her hair, and I pull it out. She looks up at me; again, we do that staring thing.

"Hi," I say, my voice sounding small. God, I felt like a teen instead of the centuries-old Sup man I am.

"Hi," she replies, and her hand moves toward my hair. She grabs something and withdraws her hand to show me its glass.

My Dragon smiles, loving how attentive she is.

"Oh, my Goddess, you guys are so cute!" Pam squeals, and my attention turns to her.

I jump suddenly, noticing a shape made of shadows against the back wall that resembles a man. Still plucking glass from my hair, Luna stops and turns to where my gaze has landed.

I ask, "What is that?"

"That's what I saw in the mirror, but it wasn't a man—just a shadow." Grabbing my chin, she moves my head so that I'm looking at her. My Dragon moans, loving her aggressiveness. "You can see it now?"

Just as quickly, her hands move back to her side, and I can no longer see the shadow-man. Wait... Is me finding my mate slowly driving me mad? How is it that one moment I can see the shadow-man and the next, I can't? My Dragon chuckles, amused at my confusion. I notice her soft but cold hands are exploring my face and the shadow-man reappears.

Wait a minute. Gently, I take both her wrists and pull them away from my face.

She gasps. "Sorry, I don't know what came—"

"It's okay," I assure her with a smile, and just as I thought, no longer can I see the shadow-man. I don't know if it's because she's my mate, but her touch allows me to see what she does. "When you touch me, I see what you see."

"Freaks!" she blurts out and shakes her head. "What I mean is, we're both freaks."

"No." I gently grip her face. "We're both Supernatural."

Luna swallows. "I can't believe you're real. I just thought you were a very vivid dream," she whispers.

I get ready to ask what she means just as my Dragon growls, telling me to pay attention. I turn my head, noticing the shadow running full speed toward us. Stepping in front of me, Luna extends both her hands, shielding me.

"What are you—"

"Return!" she screams.

An electrical current runs through my body, forcing a small jump out of me as I hear a faint yell and the shadow disappears. The rest of the lights flicker on, courtesy of the backup generator; Human magic, I believe.

"Oh, my Fairy Goddess," Pam exclaims.

Our heads turn in her direction and see what appears to be a Human male swaying left and right. However, his clothes look outdated, caked with dried dirt, and covered in holes where maggots have made their nests, many of which are crawling around on the floor.

"You have no business here." I step forward, maneuvering around Luna's petite body.

The Human turns and I pause in mid-step, not expecting the sight in front of me. There's a golf ball-sized hole where his left eye should be but no visible blood and his face is pale with decay. It truly is a terrible sight. My Dragon lifts his head as smoke puffs out of his mouth.

"Hggh," the creature moans and begins a slow, stumbling stalk toward me.

"Don't let it touch you!" my mate exclaims, and her soft hands are on my arm, pulling me toward her.

I suddenly notice the dozen translucent heads inside the holes in his body. "What the hell is that?"

"An animated corpse, or zombie," Luna replies, "and the faces inside the holes of his body are the many souls fighting for dominance."

I have no words.

She approaches the undead and takes a deep breath, one hand on its shoulder. "I release you," she says with a sigh. "I release you all."

The zombie shakes uncontrollably before it drops to the ground. Luna falls to her knees as well, panting heavily.

"We need," she pauses to catch her breath, "to burn the body." Clumsily, she reaches into her pocket. "No body means no souls can occupy it."

She pulls out a lighter and flicks it twice before a flame appears before quickly disappearing. My Dragon turns up his nose, disliking her use of another form of fire. My mouth shifts into his snout and fire spews in the zombie's direction, burning him to ash before the flames burn out, leaving nothing but embers.

"What are you?" she asks as she allows me to help her up. There's a sheen of sweat over her forehead, and her chest visibly rises and falls. She's exhausted herself from doing whatever she did with the zombie.

"A Dragon, and a powerful one," Pam replies.

Again, I turn in her direction with a glare.

"You aren't a Dragon," Luna replies with a snort. "I mean, you don't look like a Dragon."

My Dragon smiles, wanting me to show her our true form.

"That's because *this* is his Human form. He gets a lot bigger, with scales, sharp teeth, a tail, wings—the whole nine yards."

My Dragon rolls his eyes at Pam's commentary. Luna's head tilts and she stares at me again. It definitely isn't the love-of-my-life stare from earlier, but a who-is-this-man stare.

"There's no way you're a Dragon. Like, seriously," Luna says without looking at me, her attention elsewhere. "Shit!" she murmurs. "We're under attack."

Rushing past me, she moves toward the door behind us and pushes it closed. Zombies, not one, but many, push against it from the other side. There seems to be a tug of war happening, and the door staggers between them both. My Dragon growls, reminding me to get off my ass and help our mate. As I make my way over to her, I notice the gap in the doorway widening, the dead overpowering and pushing her backward. One zombie has a handful of her hair, yanking her toward him.

"Ouch!" she whines.

Wrapping one of my hands around her waist, I go to grab her hair, but she pushes me away. Surprisingly, the zombies overpower me, *me*, and pull us both into the hallway. What? How?

"Do *not* touch the animated corpses or let them touch you." Without missing a beat, Luna, using her butt, backs me into the corner wall of the dimly lit hall, shielding me. My Dragon laughs, finding her protecting me amusing.

"You will stop doing that," I respond, irritated that she finds the need to shield me.

Sighing, she whispers, "Most people would thank me for putting myself between them and a few dozen ghosts who could take control of their body."

"I am not *most* people."

Tilting her head back, she rolls her eyes before meeting mine. "Even if you're a Dragon—"

"There's no 'if' I am a Dragon..."

"You still can be possessed, and I don't want that to happen to you."

My Dragon smirks, loving that she cares for my safety. I haven't had anyone to care about me in a while and even though it will take some time to get used to it, I like that she does.

Luna clears her throat. "I have to release their souls."

She holds out her hand and takes a step forward. If she does what she did earlier, she won't survive. Wrapping an arm around her waist again, I pull her back to me. Her back collides with my front, hard. My Dragon growls, reminding me to be gentle with our mate.

"You will do no such thing!" I tell her.

A zombie snatches her away and I snatch her back.

"This won't end until their souls are freed!" she argues.

"Yes, and who will come to free your soul, after you die, because you're overexerting yourself?"

She looks up at me and blinks. "The Angels."

My Dragon rolls his eyes at the mention of them. "No!" I say, hoping my word is final.

"Fine. Do you think Pam could help me send them back?"

There's a suggestion I can get behind. "Yes."

Luna turns, her front now flush against mine. For a moment, I'm taken aback. I was not expecting this so soon and not now. Her hands gently explore my chest with a knowing smile before moving up my neck, caressing my cheek, and outlining my nose before stopping at my lips. Mentally, I prepare myself for her, for our kiss. Instead, she tilts my head and lifts my top lip, her attention locked there. What is she doing?

My Dragon lifts his head, wondering as well.

Suddenly, she thrusts her palm in my mouth and presses down on my lips. I jerk my head backward, hitting the wall behind me, and smack her ass, hoping that will stop her. My mate gasps but smirks before blushing. Oh, Father... did she like that? And why is it turning me on?

"You—"

"I didn't."

Luna shakes her head just as another zombie pulls her backward and I snatch her back toward my chest.

"Stop with the tug of war," she yells and looks over her shoulder. "I need you to bite me."

"B-bite..." I stammer. "*Bite* you?" I slap her hand away as she moves it toward my mouth again. "I'm a Dragon, not a Vampire."

"My blood will stop the zombies from taking possession of you."

"We—"

"Listen, I'm not asking. I am telling you." She sticks her hand in my mouth and grips my face tightly as a zombie pulls her away again. I snatch her back. "Now bite me!" Using both hands, she squeezes my cheeks together. My Dragon laughs, fascinated by the display. "Bite me, Cairo!"

She squeezes my cheeks harder. I can only stare because this is ridiculous. I just met my mate and now she's forcing me to bite her. I haven't bed nor kissed her, but I'm expected to bite her? Tired of this, I snatch her hand and bite, my sharp teeth easily piercing her soft flesh. I watch her reaction and she doesn't wince. *Tough girl.* The taste of copper fills my mouth and I cringe mentally.

Grabbing my hand, she pulls me behind her. I do not have time to express my dislike for my mate walking face-first into danger and pulling me behind her like a rescued damsel. As we amble through the zombies, their hands roam over both our bodies, but my Dragon's soul remains intact. Luna was right.

Pam is inside the office, standing on top of a desk, protected by her magical bubble. Each time a zombie touches the bubble, it bounces off it, falls to the ground ghostless, and pops up, reanimated once again. In her coven, she is known as a defensive Witch. Needless to say, her powers are not combative. Protection spells, bubbles, and potions are her specialty.

"Hey!" Luna shouts.

The zombies advancing on Pam stop at once before turning around heading to us. Luna releases my hands and backtracks, and the zombies mindlessly follow after her. Quickly, she runs back in and slams the door shut and then pulls out a salt shaker from her pocket. *How did she conceal that there?* Curious, I watch as my mate sprinkles salt in front of the door while dripping her blood on top of it.

"That will hold them for the time being." She turns to Pam. "Here. You need my blood so they won't take over your body."

I grab her arm. "I will not allow that," I tell her.

"But if I don't then —"

"It's fine, Ms. Luna. It's against our customs to take your blood, considering who you are to Cairo."

Pam looks at both of us with a knowing smile. When we survive this, she's fired.

CHAPTER 5

LUNA

"Pam, if you do not—"

"Who am I to Cairo?" I ask, interrupting Cairo, because it's apparent she knows something. "Whatever it is, that's the reason I've been dreaming of him, right?"

"You dream of him, do you?" Pam says, smiling ear to ear and looking at Cairo. Cairo glares in response. He does that often around her. "Your Excellency is most powerful indeed."

There goes that "Excellency" word again. "Why do you keep calling him that?"

"Cairo is—"

"Never mind all of that!" Cairo says, his voice firm. "She will *not* give you her blood." His attention turns to me. "In the future, you will refrain from offering your blood."

Bossy much? I don't go around offering my blood to everyone. I pause to think about it and realize I actually do. Oops.

Ghost 101: #6—Ghosts can body swap with any living person and Supernatural, I assume, since they are technically alive, except me. I don't know why, but there is something in my blood that prevents them from doing so. Of course, there's a way around this, as there is with almost everything in life. If I grant the ghost my permission to body swap, only then are they able to do so. I was tricked into discovering that.

"We are going to figure out a way to deal with this," Cairo continues as his attention cuts to the door, "so this night can end."

"I have a plan," I tell him. I knew what to do the moment I came in here. In a whisper, I add, "But you won't like it."

He frowns. I suppose he heard me. His eyes change colors again, his grey coloring to gold. It appears his eyes do that when he's upset.

"You are not doing anything that resembles releasing their spirits!" he states.

"So you heard me?"

"Dragons have superb hearing," Pam comments.

"You're *really* a Dragon, huh?" I ask for what feels like the fifth time tonight.

He throws his hands in the air. "Why is that so hard to believe? You can see ghosts, for—" Cairo shakes his head. "You know what? I digress."

"I don't think she's familiar with our realm, Your Excellency."

Ignoring them both, I encircle the perimeter of the room in salt.

"What are you doing?!" Cairo yells and rushes up to me.

His pupils have lost their natural shape, turning long and oval—animalistic. I suppose he is a Dragon. If Riyah was here, she would tell me to accept it and move on. But I still don't see how his tiny body can transform into a Dragon. I just can't picture it.

"You promised me you would not release their souls."

"I didn't," I reply as I use my blood to go over the salt.

Ghost 101: #7—Salt is a great medium for keeping ghosts out of your home or entrapping them. However, the older the ghost, the less effective the salt. Now, salt mixed with my blood? No ghost can overpower that.

"Fine. I embellished the promise part of the conversation, but you said you would not do it."

Honestly, I couldn't even if I wanted to. The animated corpse with the maggot-infested holes that's now a pile of ash took a lot out of me. He had fifteen ghosts fighting for dominance over his corpse body.

"Instead of releasing their souls, I'm sending them back to their places of death."

Ghost 101: #8—There are two options to rid yourself of ghosts. You can release their souls. That means sending their souls to what I call the waiting room, where a reaper will guide them to what's next. Heaven or Hell, that is. I can do this both voluntarily and involuntarily. Voluntary usually means the ghost has accomplished their unfinished business and their spirit is at peace, so they ascend by themselves. Involuntary is me forcing the release, which hurts like hell for them and tires the hell out of me. Sending them back to their places of death is what I did with Riyah earlier. That can also be both voluntary and involuntary as well. Usually, it's always involuntary and not permanent, but it requires less of my energy. It's my go-to.

"Will that require you to use your body as a conduit?"

I turn to gawk at him. How did he figure that out? That my body, my very essence, is a conduit? I open my mouth to say something but don't, hoping he drops it, but I know he won't. Instead, I start moving the furniture around the room, clearing a straight path for the ghost. Cairo steps in front of me. I stop to look up at him but notice his hands shaking. Noticing my attention on them, he balls them into fists.

"I am asking you; please, do not do this. Do not sacrifice yourself in this way—"

"Cairo, I—"

"I've just found..." He clears his throat, and I want to shake him so he'll finish that statement because I know somehow it will explain whatever this is between us and why I've been dreaming of him. But instead, his hands engulf mine and all he says is, "Please, Luna."

If my dreams of him are anything to go by, he's not the pleading type, so I know doing this is foreign to him. It makes me smile, knowing that.

"I'll be fine. Yes, it will tire me, but not as much as releasing their souls."

He pulls me closer to him, our chests touching. He's so warm. It's comforting.

"Let's take our leave," he says, his cheeks turning rosy. "Leave these ghosts to the Angels."

"Your Excellency!" Pam exclaims.

"What do you say, Luna? You and I." He rolls his eyes. "Pam, too, of course."

I release his hands as I take a step back, putting some distance between us. "You don't understand," I say with a sigh. "Ghosts talk, and if I allow these corpses who are possessed with multiple ghosts to continue, they'll possess all the Humans in the police department, if not the block, and then they'll inform other ghosts to do the same. Before long, Texas will be a ghost town, where nothing living will survive."

The reapers would also hold it against me since it disrupts the order and whatnot.

"That's his plan," Cairo says, staring in the distance.

Suddenly confused, I ask, "Whose plan?"

"Schedule an emergency meeting with the royals for tomorrow morning," Cairo orders Pam, glancing in her direction.

"Your Excellency... all of them?"

"No, only the three," Cairo replies, and Pam leaves. He turns his attention back to me. "You have my support." Wow, he's changed his mind pretty quickly. "Do what you need to do, and afterward, we need to talk."

Usually, when a guy says he needs to talk, it means he wants to break up with you.

"Okay," I reply, wondering what the talk could be about as I grab a towel and begin wiping the blood and salt from the door. Did I do something? I pause and then jump. Cairo is directly behind me. He does that often, appear by my side when he thinks danger is near. Scared me half to death!

"Make sure you stay in that room, Pam, behind the line of salt and blood."

Corpses using more strength than I will ever have push the door open, and all thirty of them rush in. Quickly, I close the door behind us and add more salt and blood. I look around the room, taking in the various souls occupying the animated corpses' bodies. There has to be about sixty, with five or six occupying each body—a big no-no in the ghost world.

Ghost 101: #9—Ghosts typically do not like sharing a living or undead body. If multiple ghosts share a body, it means they were all equal in terms of power or have been dead around the same time. If you see a single ghost in one body, he's extremely powerful and has been dead for centuries.

I stroll to the middle of the room where all the zombies are mindlessly walking around.

My mind goes back to the first time I did something like this, the fear I felt from it. How my skin crawled from their cold, dead, decaying flesh and the dead souls of the ghosts inside them, trying but miserably failing to body-swap into mine. Just because they couldn't do it doesn't mean they didn't try. Each tug, each pull, I felt in my soul; it left me cold, numb. I hated the feeling.

I jump again when I feel a warm hand on my back and look up into Cairo's eyes.

"I am here for support," he says with a nod. "Do not tell me to leave, because you forced me to consume your blood. I will be fine."

Not knowing what to say, I shrug as they descended upon me, their filthy hands reaching out to us, tugging, trying to pull me toward them. Yet warmth—a comfortable warmth, Cairo's warmth—replaces the chilly feeling. Startled by it, I turn to look at him again.

"What's the matter?" he questions, his voice laced with concern. "Do you feel faint?"

Quickly, I shake my head and turn around. Facing the zombies, my eyes suddenly water. I don't know why I have the urge to cry. I always assumed I had to get used to the cold, that I would have to deal with the ghosts all alone, and now I realize I don't.

"Return!" I yell.

I ignore the combination of screams and profanity as the corpses drop to the floor, shaking as the ghosts leave their bodies and they become nothing more than corpses once again.

"Don't forget to burn them," I say, breathing hard.

I lean over, about to fall face-first, when I feel a solid body against me. I look up into Cairo's eyes. My eyes feel heavy, but just before they close, I reach out a hand to touch his face. I want to say something before our time together ends. I don't know where I'll be when I wake. He could leave me at the police station. I mean, the man doesn't know me, and us having a... "whatever" to each other doesn't change that.

"Please find whoever killed Za'Riyah. She said not to trouble you because it wasn't her place, but I'm asking you on my behalf, Cairo."

I close my eyes and before I drift off, I hear, "Consider it done."

THE SMELL of something sweet and musty stirs me from my deep slumber. All at once, last night's events race through my mind like a slideshow, from meeting Riyah, discovering I'm not Human, going to the Supernatural police station, meeting Pam—a Witch!—dealing with animated corpses, and meeting Cairo. I roll on my side, bringing my knees to my chest. He's real. The man I've been dreaming about is *real*.

"You didn't have to send me away, you know. I would have been fine."

Oh, yeah. I did do that, but it was for her own good, mind you. But do I get a thank you? No.

"Do you hear me?" Riyah says, shaking me.

"Unfortunately," I reply and rise, wincing as a terrible headache appears, courtesy of returning all of those ghosts to their places of death, no doubt. "It was a good thing I sent you back, believe me." I stretch, finally able to place the fragrance; lavender and frankincense.

"Did Her Excellency sleep well?" a timid voice says.

I scream, backing up in the bed, expecting to hit the floor any second, but don't. What? Why? Realization hits me. This isn't my small full bed or room. Where am I?

"Riyah," I whisper, turning my head left to right, unable to pinpoint her because of the overwhelming darkness of the room.

"Who else is here?" I say with a much steadier voice. "Riyah! I *said*, who else is here?"

Her response is a giggle. I swear I'm not helping her find her killer anytime soon.

"My apologies, Your Highness," the same voice replies as the whooshing sound of fabric being pulled on a tight string fills the room before it's enveloped in light.

Clutching the sheet close to my body, I blink as my eyes adjust to the brightness. *Whose room is this?* I wonder as my eyes scan the room, taking it all in. Why is everything so... gold?

Full-length windows fill the entire length of the wall where a woman—Fairy, I assume—with wings similar to Za'Riyah's but pink, is busy separating sixteen panels. I watch as she quickly collects each red window panel and flips the thick but silky fabric at the tail, revealing dark green underneath it. Using her wings, she's airborne as she pulls the shimmering gold hanging valance in the middle, patting it ever so gently. I take notice of the balcony in the middle of windows four and five where a gold rail sits.

A past dream surfaces. Cairo is outside on the balcony, talking, but I can't remember what about. My hands are wrapped tightly around his waist and my head rests on his back, smiling as I respond to whatever he says.

This is his room, his... What does he—well, *they*—refer to it as? It's a name he loathes. I can't remember it.

I turn my attention back to the room itself; the walls are gold, a gold that shimmers when the sunlight streaming in from the windows hits them. In my dream, there is a beautiful crystal makeup vanity with a nice mirror and lights that change colors and a swivel faux fur chair. I smile as another recent dream appears, of him unsuccessfully trying to build it. Now sits a large painting of the sky during sunset and next to it are two large closed translucent doors with gold, green, and red designs. His and her restrooms are behind those doors with his and her closets as well.

In the middle of the room sits a large plasma TV that disappears when not in use. Two additional doors, similar to the bathroom doors, sit to my left, which leads to the hallway. Even though his room would make any celebrity envious, it always felt empty to me. I recall him saying his mother decorated it. She, of course, wanted to add more, but he told her no. He always told me it was my job to make our room feel like home. From my dreams, I made a few changes, but I never changed the bed.

The California king bed rests on top of a marble platform with a gold square pattern; every other pattern alternates between green and red. On all four corners sit a Dragon, colored gold, red, and green. The pillow cloth headboard is red with gold trimmings and light green designs. Gold silk bed sheets lay on top of me and red and light green decorative throw pillows are scattered around. I look up and frown as a spectacular gold chandelier hangs from the middle of a mirrored ceiling, with alternating silk red and green drapes. The things we did underneath that mirror bring a blush to my face. Riyah pinches me, and I turn to her with a glare.

"I've been calling your name for the last two minutes," she says with a roll of her eyes.

"Just like I was calling your name when I asked you to tell me who else was in this room."

She points to the glass ceiling. "Look up."

I roll my eyes, not understanding why she wants me to do that when I was just looking up there. "What is the point of..."

I lift my head to look up at the mirror but pause, just now

noticing myself. My once brown and black hair is fully silver, and it's long, longer than it's ever been. A year ago, I cut it to my shoulders but it's to my breasts now; straight and thick. If that wasn't strange in itself, I look different, too, like those Snapchat filters that beautify you. Gone are the sometimes dark circles under my eyes. My eyebrows are arched without a hair out of place, even that trouble piece that seems to have a mind of its own. My eyes seem clear, glossy, and my brown eyes seem browner, like two shining pools of hot cocoa. My nose, crooked from when I broke it as a child, appears straighter. My cheekbones are more pronounced and my skin is flawless; even my lips are red. I continue staring because I honestly don't have words.

"Why do I look...?" I turn to Riyah, noticing she also looks like a popular Snapchat filter. Grabbing a hold of my hair, she gazes at it intensely.

"All Supernaturals look like this. It's like our beauty is on crack. Us Supernatural women don't look to Humans or each other when it comes to our standard of beauty. Instead, we look up to Snowflake."

Yes, Snowflake. She's very important on Earth. The word "beautiful" doesn't do her justice. She's also the first female Angel and a warrior.

"There's someone here in Faeven with hair this same color."

"There is?"

"Yes, but I..." She trails off and drops my hair. She doesn't remember. Ghost memory sucks.

"Good morning, Miss Excellency. He did not think you would be up this early," the maid says again.

"Where is Cairo?"

"Wait, how did you figure out this is Cairo's room?" Riyah asks.

"His Excellency is currently meeting with the rulers of Faeven, Miss Luna. I've been told to assist you in whatever you may need this morning." I nod. "Shall you indulge in breakfast first or a nice hot aromatherapy bath?"

Riyah grabs both of my cheeks and turns me to face her.

"My father may be here, and I need to speak with him—" I open my mouth, but she stops me. "Please, Luna, it's very important."

CHAPTER 6

CAIRO

"Will you tell us now why you've summoned us here so early?" Vickie says, stretching loudly. My Dragon rolls his eyes, annoyed by her antics, as am I. "Or are we to wait until after you've had your breakfast?"

Setting my tea down, I look at each one of them individually. "I believe I know what Alastair is up to."

Vickie gasps and Stef snorts before getting up and moving to my wet bar. I quickly recap everything that happened last night, leaving out one key detail—Luna. They don't need to know about her. Not yet anyway.

Stef growls and yells, "Why won't you do something?!" He chunks the glass across the room, shattering it into a million pieces. "You expect us to risk our necks, our children's necks, while you sit on your ass and do nothing."

"You are out of line," Max says as he rises to his feet.

"I would have to say I rather agree with you, Stephen," Vickie interjects. My Dragon lifts his head, surprised by her confession. She and Stephen have never agreed, even when they were sleeping with each other. "You know, and yet you do nothing. Cowardly behavior."

Stephen raises the decanter in the air. "Coward indeed."

He takes a long sip and burps. Max looks at me and apologizes. I sigh. Over the centuries, I've become accustomed to their behavior, so I take no offense to any of it. At least I have one of them on my side. Max and I formed a friendship half a century ago, which I now appreciate.

"Need I remind you all that my job as your sovereign is only to intervene when absolutely necessary or after a unanimous vote." Vickie smacks her lips. "Which, as you all are aware, was none of my doing, but yours, to keep me from interfering in your mundane affairs."

My Dragon shakes his head, remembering it well.

"You can't possibly be saying this is our fault," Vickie says with a wave of her hand.

"I am, and it is. When I had control, you complained and rebelled, and then sentenced me to live in the sky." My Dragon, still upset with their treachery, latches on to my emotions, his hatred warming me. "Now you need me!" A deep growl escapes my mouth. "Now you want me to bend the very rules *you* made to keep me under your thumb."

Smoke fills the air, darkening the room.

"No need to be so snippy about it," Vickie whispers, waving her hand again but this time to clear the smoke from her view. "We remember. We were there," she says in her normal voice.

I suppose if they die, we'd finally rid ourselves of them and Faeven would gain new rulers—their children. At hearing that thought, my Dragon shakes his head. Their children are worse than they are; entitled, bratty, lazy between the two. Their parents would be my choice. Understanding, my Dragon settles down, becoming mute again and merely observing.

"Yes; remember, you need a unanimous vote. So far, that vote is four to five. The Dwarf Queen, the Flores King, the Dragon King, the Troll King, and the Queen Witch do not want King Alastair off the throne."

"Only because they know the crown will fall to his eldest son, who is like him in every way," Victorian comments.

I hold up my hand. "Nevertheless, that is the law you made, so I cannot intervene until there is a unanimous vote."

"Are we to sit here and twiddle our thumbs while this idiot takes over the realm with ghosts?" Stephen questions.

"No." I shake my head and smile. "There is a way around the laws you all created. I want you to use your wits."

"Whatever do you mean?" Max questions.

I open my mouth, ready to respond, when a bright, blinding light flashes in the room. My Dragon rolls his eyes, knowing what Supernatural the light belongs to. They are a very dramatic race. Red fire replaces the light, and Flame, with his red, blue, silver, green, and purple hair, appears. My Dragon comments the hair makes him look like a sissy, and I couldn't agree more.

"I hope I'm not interrupting," Flame speaks with intended sarcasm.

Vickie sighs dramatically, fanning herself.

"Hello, Queen Victoria." He turns his head, not his body, to spare a glance at her. The Angels are a paranoid bunch, always on edge. "My, oh my, how enchanting you are."

Correcting her posture, she straightens herself and crosses her legs, revealing toned, ebony legs and puffs out her chest. Stef snorts.

"It's not every day an Angel with a reputation, beauty, and power like yours visits us lowly Fae folk."

"I apologize for my lack of presence, but I'm not welcomed here," he turns his attention back to me, smirking, "which I find ironic, considering my son visits this castle in the sky at his leisure."

"I hold no love in my heart for you, Flame, as my brother does for your son, Blaze. Remember that." My Dragon nods, agreeing with me. "Next time, use the front door."

"No," he replies, casting his gaze around the room before landing on Stef. "Stephen, I do want to offer my sincerest condolences for losing your daughter, Za'Riyah."

Stephen glances up from his glass and blinks, surprised, as I'm sure everyone in the room is. Flame normally wears a blank face. He is not an emotional person.

"Thank you," Stephen replies, staring into the glass again.

Flame turns his attention back to me. "Get accustomed to this—"

"Accustomed to what?" I question, genuinely confused. What is he going on about?

"To me showing up unannounced." He puts air-quotation marks around "unannounced." "Luna has promised her service to the southwest region of Earth, so you will see more of me."

My Dragon roars, and in a blink of an eye, I'm on my feet. My eyes have shifted into my Dragon reptilian form, and the room looks red. Flame is standing in a cocoon of water, unbothered.

Max approaches me but stares at Flame. "What is going on?"

"You placed her in servitude? You placed my mate in *servitude*?!"

Smoke fills the room.

"Mate?!" Max and Vickie question.

"Calm down, I can't talk to you when you're in your overgrown lizard form," Flame says.

"Overgrown lizard?" I reply.

Another spew of fire fills the room.

"I'm your mate?"

Luna's voice... Her once brown and black hair is silver and gathered into a messy bun. She's wearing a silver floral-accented dress with sheer black sleeves. My Dragon pauses and stands there, embarrassed.

"That explains the dreams, and, um, I... I guess you really are a Dragon."

Her eyes travel around the room and mine follow. I notice the burnt curtains, scorched walls and floors. The head maid is definitely going to have my head if Luna doesn't maim me first for not disclosing this piece of information. I was eventually going to tell her, but not like this.

"What happened, Luna?" Flame questions as he approaches her.

Still upset, I come up behind him and step in between them, blocking his view of her. "Starting now, you don't talk to her—"

"Cairo!" my mate exclaims, trying to unsuccessfully move me out of the way.

"That's mature," Flame comments dryly.

"Whatever debt she may owe you, whatever contract she signed, I contest it."

"I see, but unfortunately," Flame sighs in a bored tone, "that is beyond my control. You need to request an audience with Ezekiel, but until then, Luna is still in service to us, and she has a job to do. Am I understood, Luna?" He looks around me.

"Yes. I'll text you the details of what happened and possibly some ideas to prevent it from happening in the future." My Dragon snorts, annoyed she's speaking to him. I turn on her with a glare. She returns it with her own and a roll of her eyes. "I think it would be best if you left, Flame. I don't want my *mate*," she says with venom but it brings a smile to my face nonetheless, "going Dragon and setting the room on fire again."

"Text me immediately!" Flame demands, and just as he appeared, he leaves in a trail of fire. Angel bastard.

"Luna..." I turn, desperate to talk about this revelation, but she's no longer behind me. Instead, she's making her way toward Stephen.

"So he's your father?" She's looking to her side, no doubt talking to Za'Riyah's ghost. "You resemble him, Riyah."

"Be careful, there's broken glass!" I warn her.

She glances down before maneuvering around it. "What is his name?" she asks Za'Riyah. "His name is Daddy to you, but I can't call him that." She sighs. "Riyah, just tell me your father's name!" she hisses and slams her hands on her hips. "No, I don't have an attitude because I found out that Cairo is my mate." She snorts as Max clears his throat.

I turn in his direction, noticing him and Vickie smirking. I'm never going to hear the end of this.

"Just mind your business and tell me his name." She throws her hands in the air. "Yes, finally!"

"King Stephen..." Luna begins as he takes another sip. He spares a glance her way before turning his attention back to the decanter. Luna takes a step forward, and it appears as if she wants to take another but decides against it; wise woman. My Dragon nods, sitting up on alert.

"I will not have words with you." He chuckles darkly. "You're probably as crazy as your—"

"You will watch your damn mouth in my home!"

He, nor anyone, Human or Supernatural, will treat her less-than with me around.

"Well!" Max says with a smile full of teeth.

"Oh, my! Things are getting interesting around here," Vickie comments, amused. "I do hope I survive it and don't die a very dreary death, so I can see how this concludes."

"Will you shut up, Vickie?" Stef snarls, his drink spilling as he carelessly waves the decanter around.

"Listen to me or not, but I'm only doing this because your daughter, Za'Riyah, who's really annoying, like seriously annoying, wants to speak to you," Luna says, turning Stephen's attention back to her.

"Oh, she's talking to a ghost," Vickie comments, nodding. "Here I thought Cairo's mate was clinically insane."

"She wants you to know she didn't mean it." She turns to Za'Riyah and mouths, *mean what*. "She said she," Luna tilts her head as her lips pucker as if she's deep in thought, "didn't mean to call you an unfaithful bastard." Luna mouths, *wow*. "She understands sometimes the heart wants what it wants, and you wanted Queen Victoria." Luna stops speaking and slowly turns her head, her gaze landing on Vickie, who huffs. Again, she mouths, *wow*. "Oh, there's more." Luna turns her attention back to Stephen. "She wants to add that she still loves you and will always watch over you, Mom, and her brother." Luna smiles. "She's crying now."

She moves her hand in circular movements on Za'Riyah's back. Stephen puts the decanter down and moves toward Luna so fast that it scares the hell out of me, so I move as well. When he wraps his arm around Luna, rests his head on her shoulder, and bawls like a baby, none of us say anything.

"I miss you too, bunny, and I love you, too," he says between sobs.

Luna, using her other hand, rubs his back soothingly. "Let it out, the both of you. Crying is good for the soul." She looks between Za'Riyah and Stephen and then steals a look at me. We share a smile.

"Cairo, come closer," Luna demands.

I obey, like an excellent mate. My Dragon chuckles at how obedient I am. "Are you about to chastise me about you finding out you are my mate?"

"Yes." She sighs. "No, I don't know." Her attention is on me, but she's still trying to console Za'Riyah and Stephen. "I think I sort of knew, if that makes sense. I..." She glances around, giving something, or rather someone else, her attention. "Bend down, I need to whisper something to you."

"I wonder what she will say?" Vickie says, intrigued. Nosey ass.

"What's wrong?" Luna turns to Za'Riyah, or at least I think so because nothing else is there. "No, don't you ghost-freeze on—and she's froze."

The door bursts open and my head maid rushes in. "The Necromancer's son, Prince Landon, is here."

She looks at me with wide eyes and makes quick glances at Luna. Fuck!

"Thank you, Miss Justice. Offer him a *refreshment*," I stress, hoping she'll read between the lines. He must take a refreshment. He cannot refuse.

"You were about to tell me something," Luna says, continuing her conversation with Za'Riyah. "Of course you've forgotten. I think you were experiencing your death again, Za'Riyah." She smiles as she shoulder-bumps her. "Don't worry; we'll get to the bottom of it." Her attention is back on me. "I really need to tell you this."

More aggressively than needed, I pull Stephen from Luna. He drops to the floor and balls himself up, sobbing heavily. This is a good release for him, but I don't have time to comfort him as he grieves. Not at the moment. I have to protect Luna.

"You need to hide," I tell her as I pull her gently toward the wall.

"Hide where? What's going on?" Luna questions.

I can't explain, not now, but I will. I just don't have the time.

"He can't see you. Just wait here and I will explain later, I promise." Running my hands over the wall, I locate a loose stone and press it. A secret passage opens up and I turn to glare at the others in the room. "If any of you speak about this passage, I will kill you."

"I do not think he can threaten us this way," Vickie comments.

"Yet he did," Max says.

"You want me to hide in there, in the dark? Cairo, come on! This is—"

"I don't have time, really, just stay here and I'll come get you in a few, I promise."

"But Cairo, I need to tell you—" She tries to push against me. "It's important, and if I tell you this, my hiding wouldn't be—" Using more force, I push her. She stumbles a little and glares at me because of it. "I swear if you close that—"

"You won't be in there long, not even five minutes," I reassure her and close the passageway. My Dragon chuckles, knowing I'm going to hear a mouthful about this later.

Quickly I make my way to the wet bar, step over Stephen, and pour myself a drink as Prince Landon comes in, looking every bit like his father.

"Father was right! You are meeting in secret," Prince Landon says as he takes a seat next to Vickie. "Don't you look lovely today, Queen Vickie?"

She snorts and turns to face Max. "Don't patronize me. We both know I'm not your type."

Prince Landon snickers. Yes, snickers.

"Yes, yes, I suppose that is true." He smiles. "But you can

convince me otherwise." He uses his fingertip and trails it down her neck.

"Oh, my goodness!" she exclaims and gets up, taking a seat closer to Max, where Stephen usually sits.

"As I told your father, I do not take well to you appearing here, uninvited."

Landon snorts and crosses his ankles. "Your threats mean nothing to me or my father. We both know you have no true power."

"You believe so?" I question, and I know my eyes shift before they shift back. "Answer me this, young Landon." I swirl the liquor in my cup. "Is a Necromancer prince useful if he's dead like the very ghost who he commands?"

He swallows and stands. "You have a female guest here, and we want her."

"If you're referring to Queen Victoria," I gesture to her, "take her. She's yours."

"Hey!" Vickie exclaims.

"No, I mean a *young* female," Landon says.

Vickie gasps. "Watch it, boy!"

"A female who looks like Mother," Landon continues.

I nod as I take another sip. "As you can see, no one is here that resembles your mother," I reply.

"As far as the eyes can see..."

He turns to the wall where I've hidden Luna and smiles. Damn it! I think that's what she was trying to tell me. There must be a ghost here who's reporting all the happenings to the Necromancer Kingdom. This is how they know about the secret meetings! My Dragon nods, agreeing. How many other ghosts are here?

"You wouldn't mind if I looked around, would you?"

"I would, and you have overstayed your welcome."

Ignoring me, he walks toward the wall. I open my mouth and a line of fire flies in his direction, scorching his shirt. He jumps back, his eyes wide.

"You... you... you can't do that!"

"I can when you were not invited here. This is my domain, and I told you she is not here."

"You're lying!" he yells, sounding like the spoiled child he is.

"You are weighing on my patience. I will not tell you again to leave, Prince Landon."

"Fine, but this is not over," he promises. "Let me remind you, she is a Necromancer, so she belongs in my father's kingdom, meaning she is subjected to the whims of her king, and he *will* see her."

He looks to the wall where I've hidden her once more before walking out. Miss Justice stands by the door.

"Please see him out."

"Yes, Your Excellency," she replies, and follows behind him, closing the door.

Quickly, I make my way to the same wall I hid Luna behind. Vickie clears her throat and I hold up my hand, silencing her because I know she's going to say something inappropriate or annoying and I don't need either. When I press the loose stone and the wall moves to the side, I find it empty. Stepping in, I look to my left and right using my Dragon vision, but I don't see her.

"Luna!" I call for her.

Where did she go? Did Prince Landon accomplish what he came here to do?

CHAPTER 7

LUNA

Cairo, my mate, pushing me in this overwhelmingly dark secret passage is so stupid. Speaking of mates, I figured we were something along those lines because of my dreams. Actually, that's incorrect. I thought I was losing my mind.

I'm glad I'm not, in fact, going crazy. Of course, I have no clue what a mate is or how a mate should behave, but that doesn't worry me. Cairo, as pushy as he is, and a tad bit destructive, seems like the perfect person to show me the ropes. I smile. Wait until I tell my sisters. They'll be so jealous, and my mom won't worry about me dying alone and childless. *Aww, family!* Actually, I probably need to check in with them, considering I didn't go home last night. Note to self: Do that later.

"You are lying!"

Prince—um... what's his name? I know it starts with an L, but I can't recall it. Anyway, he's yelling.

Yes, the prince knows I'm here because of the several ghosts in Cairo's home, and the one ghost with a scar on his neck—an Elf, judging by the shape of his ears—is present in the room they were meeting in. If I'm not mistaken, the Elf ghost is popping back and forth.

Cold, dainty hands grab my warmer ones and cause me to jump.

"Za'Riyah?" I whisper. "That's you, right?"

"Yes," she responds but doesn't give me any attitude, sarcasm, snark. Nothing.

I think she's still shaken up after freezing or having a heart-to-heart with her father. I squeeze her hand, letting her know I'm here and I care.

I lean in closer, trying to hear the exchange between them both. Prince Whatever His Name Is is adamant about seeing me, but Cairo is like, "No!" But the prince is unrelenting, and is like, "Blah blah, Necromancer, blah, blah."

Wait, Necromancer?

I mouth the word. Isn't Necromancer magic *black* magic? Am I evil? I definitely did not see this coming. I don't feel evil. Are all Necromancers in this world, this Faeven, evil?

Suddenly, a big, warm hand covers my mouth. Frightened, I try to scream, and my arm is pulled back into a hard body. Someone quickly moves us back through the overwhelming darkness. I wiggle with all my might trying to free myself, but no such luck, my captor won't release. Finally, the darkness is illuminated by light spilling from under the door. Great. As soon as my captor goes to open the door, I'll use it as a chance to escape.

"It's me, Luna! It's Leonardo," he whispers.

"What?" I hiss, confused by his sudden appearance as he drags me behind him.

I blink my eyes, adjusting to the light, finally seeing him. Riyah's hands grip my arm and she stands behind me, like a child standing protectively behind her mother. Pushing him off of me, I yell, "What is your problem?"

"Keep your voice down!"

"Keep my voice down? Keep my voice down?!" Upset, I shove him again. "You intruded in on me in that stupid dark passage, dragged me all the way down here, and now you want me to *keep my voice down?*"

"I'm sorry, Luna, really I am, but Cairo has great hearing—"

"You know Cairo?"

He mutters "fuck" before sliding his hand down his face. To think I was being courteous by sending the text message last night when he knew all along about this place. A popping sound behind me makes me turn. I know it's the Elf ghost trailing us. Hand extended, I walk into the darkness. When my hand touches something cold and sweaty, I say, "I release you!" out loud. An electric current runs through my body and the Elf releases a scream before he's gone.

"You said you were adopted as well, Leo!" I yell, making my way back to him. The door is now open. "That you didn't know who our parents were."

"I know, I know!" he replies.

"Now I find out that you know what this Faeven place is, you know who Cairo is, and no doubt you probably know who our biological parents are."

"We hail from the Necromancer community. We're the children of the great King Alastair and Queen Lilliana. Prince Landon is our brother. He's the eldest and currently next in line for the throne."

"We've known each other for five years, Leo. At any time, you could have mentioned this to me."

"I know, I know, but Mom told me not to, so I—"

Mom... the woman who abandoned me but chose to keep *both* Leo and our brother, whose name I still can't freaking remember. Fuck her.

"Luna!" Cairo's voice echoes in the hallway.

"You and *your* mom can go to hell, Leo. I'm going back."

I know Cairo would have told me about this the first chance he got. Cairo cares about my safety, cares about me. He is my mate, for freak's sake.

"There's a reason we refer to Cairo as His Majesty, His

Excellency, and not King Cairo," Leo says, shaking his head. "He's not like the rest of us. His power knows no bounds! It's not wise for you to stay here with him. If there's any other person who would kill you other than Father—"

"Wait, your father, my birth father, wants to kill me. Why? What did I do to him? I don't even know the man."

"Yes, Luna. That's why Mom sent you away." What? But *why*? "Cairo is dangerous."

"But he's been so nice to me. He's been—"

"You haven't even known him for a full day." Leo points in the hallway. "You've known me for five years and didn't know I was lying to you." Wow... that's accurate but shady. "How can you say if he's being honest with you or not? You aren't exactly the best judge of character."

I decide I will always hate Leo. Like, my children's children will talk about this betrayal and will never, ever call him uncle.

"Luna, Cairo knows the power you hold. He wants to manipulate you, I promise. Come with me. Give me a chance to explain everything. Let me make this right."

I look at Riyah, who shrugs. Leo hasn't been truthful to me, but he's always been there. Cairo and I have a genuine attraction, plus he's my mate. But in the back of my mind, I've always wondered about my birth family. This could be the closure I need so I can finally move on with my life. Swallowing, I nod, letting him know I'm in.

"Okay, let's go."

Leo suspiciously pokes his head out the door and quickly looks to his left and right before dropping to his knees and crawling through the golden—yes, golden; some glittery, some glossy—gravel. I turn back to Riyah. Because what the freak is he doing?

"Landon may still be here," she says, running her fingers through her hair.

She follows Leo, as if that explains his suddenly weird behavior. Dropping to the floor, I follow behind them. Let's add this to the list of stupid things I've done today. When Leo stops and begins pushing the gold gravel to one side, I assist. An old, wooden trap door with the remains of gold paint appears.

"I'll go first," Leo tells me, and then stands so suddenly I get whiplash.

He pulls open the door and drops through the opening. Still on my stomach, I look down, seeing nothing but clouds. Suddenly, there's a vibration against my butt, and I pat myself, trying to identify where the vibrations are coming from. My phone. Crap, who could that be? Cairo? No, he doesn't have my number. Fishing my phone out of my back pocket, I see that it's Flame's number. Impatient much?

I turn to Za'Riyah, who's messing with her hair. "I need you to go to Flame."

"What?" she pouts. "But I'll miss the family reunion."

"Yes, and I will fill you in when you return." I won't. "Tell him about the shadow that entered the police station and then tell him about the animated corpses and the ghosts who occupied them, that I returned them to their places of death."

"But," she whines, "I wasn't there for the animated corpses."

"No, but you were there for the shadow in the mirror."

Riyah looks at me, unblinking, twirling her hair. "Ugh fine, fine, fine."

"Mention the shadow thing first. Remember that's the most important thing, then mention the animated corpses and how I returned them to their place of death and Cairo burned their undead bodies."

"I have to do everything myself, don't I?" she replies, ignoring me before she pops and disappears. The moment I solve her death and get rid of her can't come soon enough.

"Jump down, I'll catch you!" Leo calls from below, reminding me about the situation at hand.

Closing my eyes, I say a quick prayer and jump. When I feel muscular arms around me, pulling me backward and settling me on my feet, I open my eyes again. The clouds are so thick I can't see Leo, even though I know he's right next to me, nor can I make out anything in front of me.

"Stay to the side," Leo says, grabbing my hand and gently pulling me after him. "I'll lead us."

"I want you to know I'm still mad at you," I tell him because he needs to understand that.

"I know. I didn't intentionally mean to lie to you, but I couldn't allow you to come here."

"You know, maybe our birth father doesn't want to kill me anymore and our brother was coming to retrieve me to apologize."

Leo snorts. "Make no mistake, Luna. Father not only wants to kill you, but he wants to bathe in your blood to absorb your power while our brother watches in hopes he can join in the festivities. Yeah, real fucking family reunion," he replies.

Well, damn. I pause my steps, digesting that my birth father and eldest brother really want to kill me. Seriously, how messed up is that? Leo tugs at me and I continue following in silence, with Leo leading the way, me clutching on to him for dear life, not wanting to fall to my death. A thought occurs to me.

"The castle in the sky?" I say out loud, and I realize that's the name everyone calls this place and Cairo hates it, or it appeared he did in my dreams.

"His Excellency chooses it to be this way."

"Huh?"

"His castle in the sky, where we're currently at. His Excellency chose it to be this way,"

That's a lie, and I don't need dreams to tell me so. No one would willingly choose isolation. No one.

An enormous green Dragon is up ahead, flapping its massive wings, clearing the surrounding clouds, revealing—you guessed it—a golden landing strip underneath connected to a steep and scary cliff. I gotta say it's scarier seeing it. One slip, and Leo and I would become the very ghosts we help.

"Is the Dragon a ghost?" I ask.

"Yes," Leo replies with a smile. "*She* is our escort from this castle in the sky, so let's go."

The Dragon nose dives just as Leo leaps off the ledge, landing on its back with a thud. He pats the Dragon affectionately and whispers something I can't hear. Knowing I'm leaving Cairo doesn't sit well with me. I sound like those women in my sister's stupid romance novels. I don't know this man, my mate, yet the thought of leaving his castle in the sky makes me sad.

"Are you coming, Luna?" Leo questions.

"Goodbye, Cairo," I whisper, and jump.

CHAPTER 8

LUNA

After a few minutes of flying, I make out a bright, sparkly town. I notice a lot of buildings the closer we get, and not traditional Human buildings, but mini castles; all different heights. Some are two, others three, some five stories high, and each a different color. Pink, orange, light blue, resembling that of a sunset in my world. As the sun hits the ground below these buildings, they sparkle silver, as if someone carelessly spilled a ton of glitter.

So that's where the sparkling comes from, I think to myself. Seriously, who built this Supernatural world?

My mouth hangs open in shock as I take in the non-Humans walking around. I see more dark Fairies, their darker wings varying in hue from rich purples, blues, black, and browns. I take notice of the other Fairies, who possess wings in lighter pastel colors.

"If the Fairies with the darker wings are 'dark Fairies,' then the Fairies with the light pastel wings are—"

"Light Fairies," Leo says, confirming my thought.

"Does dark mean bad and vice versa for the light Fairies?"

Leo shakes his head. "No, the dark Fae here are short-tempered but otherwise good. They're the warrior Fae, whereas the light Fae—

or the trickster Fae, most commonly referenced in those Human stories of yours—are the Fae that Humans should steer clear of."

I think back to Queen Victoria and the light Fae in Cairo's bedroom opening up his windows. They didn't seem bad. Well, Queen Victoria is a cheater, but still, that doesn't mean she's evil.

Elves, or so I assume by their pointed ears, perfectly contoured noses, and angular facial features, stroll by.

"Elves!" I say aloud, unable to take my eyes off a woman nearby. She's glaring at a light Fairy male, who seems oblivious to stepping on her puffy dress that looks as though it's from the Elizabethan era. "Do they all dress like that?"

Leo snorts. "No, only a group of them. It's a club."

I notice the trees and flowers are animated and moving down the street. The males, I'm assuming, resemble tree trunks. Their arms, hands, fingers, and legs are bendable branches, with an impressive height of eight feet. The hair on top of their heads resembles dreads, which hang low down their backs. Leaves cling to their tree-like bodies in the shape of tops and bottoms. Female bodies have a strong resemblance to the males, except shorter; maybe six feet. Vines with flowers circle the women's exposed arms, legs, and fingers. Instead of dreads, more vines sprout from their heads with flowers that give them the appearance of beautiful, curly hair. Leaves also cling to their bodies, resembling short to long dresses.

"What are they?" I wonder, still marveling.

A baby male, maybe five feet tall, notices us approaching and points. His mom, oblivious to him, continues shopping.

"Naturein," Leo replies as he sticks his tongue out at the baby Naturein, making him laugh before he runs toward his mother, trying to get her to focus on us. "Naturein is the species name, but the males are referred to as Radices and the females are Flores."

She finally turns her attention to us and makes a face before returning to her shopping. Now that I think about it, none of the other non-Humans seem surprised by us just floating in the sky, because that's what we're doing; they can't see the Dragon ghost we're riding on.

We land between two buildings in an alleyway—a trashy, glittering, silver-floored alleyway—where no one is around. Leo thanks the green Dragon, and she takes off into the sky.

"Here, we need to go undercover," Leo says, and I see he's holding two sealed test tubes. "Take this."

Skeptically, I take one. "What is this?"

"A spelled formula made by a Witch to hide your true appearance."

"Does it taste bad?" I ask, and then chastise myself for the question. What I should ask is will it harm me?

"No," he replies and peels the plastic off of his.

I follow suit and sniff mine. It is surprisingly floral. "Will it do anything to me?"

"Nope," he replies quickly... almost too quickly. "Bottoms up." He taps his tube against mine.

Here's stupid thing three or four I've done today. I've lost count. We both down the vials.

Smacking, I nod approvingly. "Not bad at all. Tastes like cherries, and I don't feel—" I gasp as a wave of intense abdominal cramps hits me and I fall to my knees. "Oh, my God!"

I glare at Leo, who's holding onto the wall, roughly inhaling and exhaling. A burning sensation suddenly hits my ears. I reach out toward them, wanting to rub the pain away, when another wave of abdominal pain hits me, forcing me into the fetal position. Just as quickly as the pain started, it stops. Also, my ears have stopped burning.

"I swear I'm going to literally kill you if you lie about anything else," I tell him as I get up.

"As if you would have taken it knowing there was pain," comes a voice that does not belong to Leo.

I look up and notice his hair is different. Our once-shared Coca-Cola-brown hair—before mine turned silver—has been replaced with platinum blonde hair. Leo's eyes are blue, and he has Elf ears. I reach for my own, and they feel pointy as well.

"What color is my hair?" I ask.

"Bright red," he replies.

I try to grab a piece but it is cut so short I can't grasp it. "Three hours is all we got; you'll know when it's about to wear off."

He begins walking and I follow. He stops mid-step before turning to look at me. "I'm sorry about all of this, Luna," he says suddenly, and I smile and bump my shoulder to his. I didn't realize how much I wanted an apology from him, but I guess I did. "I want to be honest." Yes, *finally.* "Even though Mom won't like it this way, I think in order to maintain our relationship, honesty is key."

I agree but sigh. "We're meeting her, our birth mother, aren't we?"

This is where he's going with this, right?

"Yes, and I didn't tell you sooner because I knew you wouldn't want to meet her."

He knows me so well. I glare, and he pretends he doesn't notice and continues walking. Finally, he stops at the door of a two-story café and gestures for me to enter. Leo points to a table where a blonde Elf is sitting, folding her napkin. She notices Leo pointing at us and smiles in our direction, waving us over. Immediately, I want to cry. She's incognito, and I want to cry. Here's another opportunity for me not to see my birth mother, the same woman who willingly gave me up. Sadness turns into anger. I realize I hate her.

"I'm going to order you a juice and breakfast sandwich," Leo tells me.

"I'll wait with you," I tell him, but he pushes me in her direction. "Go talk with her. She doesn't bite."

Yeah, but I do.

I move to my birth mom, who stands and opens her arms as if she's going to hug me but pauses, smiling before swallowing.

"Sorry. You probably don't want to hug a stranger," she says, and I couldn't agree more. I smile, even though I don't feel like it, and take the seat across from her. No way am I sitting next to her. "I know you're wondering why I gave you away."

Yes, it kept me up many nights in my adolescence. "Leo says you kept me away because the Necromancer King wants to kill me and bathe in my blood for my powers," I reply, and instantly want to take it back when her smile turns into a frown.

I didn't mean to be so upfront, but isn't it the truth? Why are we sugarcoating the truth? I'm a big girl. I can handle it.

"Getting straight to the point." She gives me a sad smile. "You're a lot like your father in that way." Since he wants to kill me and bathe in my blood, I don't take that as a compliment. Leo finally arrives with food and drinks. "Unfortunately, Luna, there's more to it."

"She's right. Way more," Leo says, apparently overhearing the convo, and takes a seat next to her.

No surprise there. I bet he's a Momma's Boy, too. I hate them both.

"It was foretold that you would be more powerful than your father, that you..."

She trails off, but Leo urges her to continue.

"Go ahead, Mom. Tell her everything. I've known Luna for five years, and she's pretty understanding."

Understanding, sure. Forgiving? Not so sure.

"I need to start from the beginning if you're going to understand any of this, Luna." I nod. "I'm not from this realm, Faeven. I'm actually from Mercury's realm. There we have Enchanters and Enchantresses... Witches, basically." She swallows. "I'm what you call a rare Enchantress. I can commune with the dead. No one else from Mercury Realm can do that. A ghost Enchantress is the terminology they gave it, but my powers do not compare with your father's. He's from Faeven, and his grandmother is a descendant of an air Angel. Your silver hair, which should have appeared when you arrived in Faeven, you got it from her."

Well, that explains the hair. I wonder if Flame knows this. Better question: Does he know who the Angel is? Is the Angel still alive?

My anger vanishes. If I'm as powerful as they think, because Angels are pretty powerful, I can sort of see why they sent me to Earth.

"I can talk to the dead, create potions and spells to keep them out of establishments or suspended in one place, but I can't send the dead to their resting place, to the afterlife, or enter the shadow place."

"Neither can I," Leo adds. "Landon can, sort of, but there are limits to his abilities, and once he uses all his gas, it takes weeks for him to recharge."

"Your power is like your father's, similar to his grandmother." Okay, now I see why they want to bathe in my blood. By doing so, they would get my power. "You're like an electrical conduit for ghosts. With a few more centuries behind your belt, who knows what you'll be capable of."

"Why not wait those few centuries to see what will become of me?" I question.

"Luna, you don't understand," Leo says, taking a bite out of his sandwich. "Currently, you and Father are equally matched regarding your powers. It took him two *centuries* to be able to send ghosts back to the afterlife, using his body as a conduit, and another century to send them to their places of death."

"And you?" I point to my birth mother and take a drink of my coffee. I make a face and look down at it, forgetting Leo has a big sweet tooth. It's nothing but creamer, sugar, and that almond milk crap. I prefer mine dark, like my birth father's soul, apparently. "You were foretold of this, and I get that, but what if the prediction—"

"Prophecy!" they both practically scream, and then look around the café to see if anyone heard them before looking at each other. I called it—Mommy's Boy!

"Fine. Prophecy!" I nod. "But what if it's wrong?"

"It's not, Luna," my birth mom states, as if her words are final.

"If you knew this, why not kill him before my birth?" I whisper. If he was such a bad person, why not end his life before I was born twenty-five years ago? "Or have someone else kill him? Maybe Cairo, or maybe one of the Angels."

Again, they look at each other.

"Why did she mention Cairo?" she asks Leo.

"She was with him when I went to retrieve her." My birth mother frowns. "I think he kidnapped her."

I look at Leo. "He did not."

"She may have Stockholm syndrome," Leo whispers to her, and she nods in understanding.

What the actual hell.

I put us back on the topic at hand. "Why couldn't you kill him or get someone to kill him?"

"I couldn't do it," my birth mother says.

Leo looks surprised. "You tried?"

"During the prophecy, the oracle said I would need to kill him in order to save you."

The anger is back. "And you couldn't do that?"

"No. He's my soulie. You only get one, and your father is mine."

She reaches out toward me as if she's going to grab my hand. Quickly, I snatch it backward, spilling my coffee on the table.

"It's okay, we're okay," Leo says loudly, looking around the room.

We've gained an audience. He grabs a colorful cloth from a rack against the wall and begins wiping up the spill. I resist the urge to kick him or throw the rest of the coffee in his face because he knew about this, too.

"He wasn't always like this. I swear, for five hundred years, we lived together peacefully," my birth mother adds, and that sends me on edge.

I rise from my chair, bumping into the table and spilling her coffee, too. "I don't care how he was then!"

"You're too loud," Leo warns and shushes me.

"Don't you shush me!" I yell, and then notice I'm making a scene. Lowering my voice, I lean in. "I am your child. I should come first. I don't care how long you've known that man." Using my butt, I push the seat backward and it falls to the floor. Do I pick it up? No.

"This conversation isn't done," she whispers. "We need to talk about him taking over the realms, including your Earth."

"I don't care," I tell her. "By the way, don't contact me ever again." I look at Leo. "You, too. The both of you are dead to me."

"Luna!" Leo whispers as he stands.

I ignore him and storm out of the café, angrily swiping at my face. The tears have started. What sort of mother does that, picks her spouse over her child, the only girl she's birthed. What type of mom does that make her? Why him and not me?

Why didn't she choose me? I wonder as I look up into the sky, my tears falling freely.

"Are you okay?" Cairo's voice sounds from behind me, and for the third time, I jump. What is up with this world scaring me? Wiping my tears, I turn to face him. He looks good in his Shaft-inspired beige coat. "Are you okay, Luna?" he asks again.

I nod. Not trusting my voice before I clear my throat, I realize something. "How..." I clear my throat and wipe my eyes again. "How did you know it was me?" He points to his nose. "I don't know what that means."

"Your smell. My Dragon tracked your smell."

I don't know if that's romantic or creepy. I take a step toward him but pause. Leo's stupid voice appears in my head, reminding me that I shouldn't trust Cairo and how he wants to use me. But didn't he and my birth mother lie to me about... Oh, I don't know, my whole life? Wouldn't they lie about this, about Cairo, too?

Cairo slowly closes the distance between us. "Why do you look like this?"

"I'm incognito," I tell him with a shrug. "It's a potion from a Witch."

"Prince Leonardo... where is he?" Cairo asks, looking over my shoulder, his nose flaring.

"In the fancy café with my birth mother," I tell him, pointing. "If you're going to kill them, make sure she suffers," I add.

"Kill!" Cairo exclaims. "What happened?"

CHAPTER 9

CAIRO

"Where are you going?" I ask, following behind her.

"Home!"

"You," my voice cracks, and I clear my throat, "you want to return home, back to your realm?"

She nods once. My Dragon, not loving the idea, shakes his head. If she leaves, will she come back? Do I want to find out?

After realizing Prince Leonardo was the one who took her in the secret passage, I didn't feel the need to rush to her rescue. They are related, and unlike Prince Landon, Leo took after their mother, Lily. I knew she wouldn't be in any immediate danger and the sooner she learned who she was, the better. Now, seeing her with puffy red eyes, I regret my decision.

"Yes!"

"What happened, Luna? What did Prince Leonardo and Queen Lilliana say to you?"

"What type of woman names all her children with the first consonant of her name? Freaking weirdo."

I chuckle because I've always thought the same thing. She stops walking and turns around, hands on her hips, glaring at me.

"What?"

"Tell me the truth, Cairo. I can't take any more secrets today."

"Okay," I reply slowly, not knowing where she's going with this. My Dragon smiles, enjoying my confusion.

"You didn't take me to your castle in the sky because you're some crazy tyrant who wants to use me for my power, right?" Taken aback, I mentally repeat her question to myself, and my Dragon starts laughing. I don't know if it's his laughter or the question itself, but it angers me.

"Why would a Dragon need ghost power?!" I yell.

"I don't know. Maybe you want to get back at the people of Faeven for banishing you to the sky," she says with a shrug.

"How do you..." Wow. "Why, yes, you've figured me out, Luna!" My Dragon closes his eyes, knowing I'm about to lose my cool. Her mouth opens wide in shock. Sups on the street have stopped walking, watching Their Excellency lose whatever remaining dignity I have left. "I'm going to drain you of your ghost power, then I'm going to attack the town with the undead."

"I knew it!" Luna says, hands still on her hip.

"If I'm going to kill the Sups of Faeven, they're going to burn, fire and brimstone." A few of the Sup watching us gasp. My Dragon shakes his head, disagreeing with me. Traitor. "Not by some stupid ghost."

"Now my power is stupid?"

"Go home, Luna." I spin and storm off. "Go home and leave me to my loneliness."

"If I go home, I'm not coming back!" she shouts from behind me.

Throwing up the peace sign, something my brother does to me often that annoys me to no end, I continue walking.

After a few moments of me calming down, I decide I've handled the situation like a child. She assumed, or better yet was possibly persuaded by her mother and brother, that I want to use her powers to enslave Faeven? I admit, at one point, I did think about it—that is, me enslaving Faeven, *not* me using her to do it—but I've moved past that. I also do not think her power of seeing ghosts is useless. However, if I was, and I'm not, going to kill the Sups of Faeven, they would burn; a fitting end for forcing me to the sky.

I should have been more understanding. She is my mate, and from the outside looking in; she knows nothing about Faeven or her family. The only genuine connection she has to our realm and her family is her ability to see ghosts. I, as her mate and a man, need to remember that and help guide her through her discovery of this place and her family.

"Cairo, you can stop following me now," she comments, pointing to a plain-looking tree.

Without any assistance from me but direction from the passing Sups on the streets, we finally made it to the closest portal. Only took us an hour to get here. Luna is hopeless when it comes to direction.

A Witch from Pam's coven sits next to it, texting on her phone. Noticing me, she quickly puts the phone away, tucking it into her bra. Her job is portal monitor, charged with checking identification cards and ensuring those entering and exiting are Sups of Faeven. In our realm, we have twelve portals, and each serves a different purpose. For example, one portal is specifically for the entrance of the arrogant Angel race, even though few use it. This portal and two others are for Faeven Sups only.

Luna gets in line, glaring at me the whole time, doing that hands on hips thing. My Dragon nods, liking what he sees.

"Your Excellency," the Witch guarding the portal whispers. She clears her throat. "Your Excellency!" she says a little louder now, confidence in her voice. "You and your friend don't have to wait in line."

The other Sups step out of the way, gesturing for us to go ahead. My Dragon nods, loving the respect.

"Thank you—"

"That's unnecessary," Luna says, glancing in their direction and smiling.

She turns behind me and cocks her head, no longer looking at me but through. I turn quickly, wondering if her brother or mother appeared yet no one is behind me. No one I can see, anyway. There's a ghost here, which doesn't surprise me because I assume they're everywhere, but Luna looks disturbed by this ghost. Why?

She chuckles before whispering, "This is not your world, this is not your world." Yet it is. Tilting her head, she looks at the sky. "So pretty."

The sun is setting, so our unnaturally blue sky is silver-gray; the glittering buildings now glowing. Eventually, the sun will set, and the silver-gray sky will give way to chocolate-brown.

"Cairo." She's looking at me now. Slowly, she crosses the distance between us. "I know you don't want to use my ghostly powers to enslave this world." I ignore the mutterings of the Sups at the word of enslavement. "Well, that's a lie." She dramatically sighs. "I want to be honest with you, and I hope you return the favor." I nod. "Heck, I just met you, but I've been dreaming about you for years now."

This is the second time, I believe, she's mentioned she dreams about me. What does she mean by that?

"I'm still accepting the fact you're real, so no; I wasn't worried about you using me, but after talking to Leo..." She rolls her eyes. "He got to me, and I'm not proud to admit that, but he did, and I'm sorry." She smiles. "I'm sorry, Cairo."

"I accept your apology." I wasn't expecting that. Women usually never admit they're wrong. I'm glad to see my mate is different.

"Can you answer this question for me, Cairo?" Again, we have an audience. We are definitely going to be the talk of the town. "Did you choose to put your castle in the sky, or did they force your hand?"

It could be me being paranoid, but I swear all the Sups step a little closer, wanting to make sure they hear the answer. Majority are Luna's age, so they do not know the truth, only stories and rumors told to them by their parents and others.

"They forced my hand," I reply between clenched teeth, not wanting to admit it out loud. But if she's being honest with me, I can be honest with her, too.

She grabs both pockets of my double-breasted overcoat and surprisingly pulls me toward her. I don't have time to reprimand her or express my surprise because she leans in, using her tiptoes, and kisses me. My Dragon blushes and I do nothing. I'm stunned she kissed me first. Again, this is not happening the way it should, and for the first time in my long life, that is okay. Luna is my mate, my one special person, and I am lucky to have finally found her.

She releases me and steps back, a smirk on her face. Smug brat and yet I would spend the rest of my life ensuring she is happy. I grab her hand, pulling her into me, my lips find hers. She giggles as she closes her eyes, running her tongue over my top lip before I take that same tongue and suck it before kissing the edge of her mouth. She giggles again. I kiss her top lip first, bottom lip second before giving her a single peck on her closed lips. The Sups clap—yes, clap—and my Dragon roars his approval. We'll be the talk of the town for weeks to come. Months maybe.

"By the way," she says, her eyes fluttering, breathing hard, "death by fire and brimstone is way cooler than a town overrun by ghosts."

I can't help myself, I smile at the mention of that. Damn right it is. Luna sighs as she reaches into her pocket and pulls out her phone, scrolling through her messages. I notice Leo's name.

Luna says, "Now they're concerned about my whereabouts. Liars."

"We need to talk about what happened with your mother and brother." She shrugs and grabs my hand, and then walks in the direction she was looking at earlier. A troll, a ghost troll, is there with a pad and pencil. Is the ghost taking notes? Ghost can do that?

"What are you doing?" she asks him.

He rolls his eyes. "I don't answer to you, Princess, nor him." He looks at me. "I'm dead, in case you haven't noticed."

"Ghosts love reminding you about them being dead," Luna whispers to herself, and I chuckle. She appears to have a love-hate relationship with them. "I asked what you were doing, and if I don't

84

get an answer, I'll send you on your way. Let the reapers deal with you."

"Do it, Missy, and you'll be on your ass for the next week, maybe months. You are a woman, and women are weak."

"Wow." I turn to look at Luna, and she's smugly smiling. "That was sexist."

"It was indeed. Yeah, I'm not like my brother or father." She takes a step closer to the troll ghost, and he takes a step back. "I'll send you back and then send a few dozen after you and be fine. And for the sexist comment, I'll talk to the reaper and make *sure* you go... " She points at the ground. Can she do that? My Dagon smiles wickedly. "Now let's try this again. What are you doing?"

He extends the notepad toward her, drops it, and takes off.

"I did not expect him to run," I comment, surprised.

"Yeah, well, they always do," she replies with a shrug and pulls out her phone.

I watch as she scrolls through her apps before clicking on one. A siren appears on the phone, but there's no sound. Suddenly, there's growling and two dogs—ghost dogs, I assume—appear out of the air. Siberian huskies. One jumps on her, licking her leg, while the other ignores her and growls at me. She reaches down and picks up the tablet, passing it to them. They sniff, even the mean one whose attention is still on me. What is this ghost dog's problem?

"Bring him back," Luna orders.

Just as they popped in, they pop out. Ghost dogs—I have to say, I did not know that was a thing. The dogs reappear with the troll. The angry one is biting his left leg while the other smiles affectionately toward Luna.

"You, you, you—"

"That's what you get for underestimating me."

"You're too late. He's already started, and you're too late."

I know who the ghost is talking about, the Necromancer King, but I don't know what he's referring to. What does he mean, we're too late?

Luna waves the notepad. "That may be true. Either way, you won't get to see how it ends." She releases my hand. Immediately, my ability to see him goes away. "I release you. Tell Flame I said hi."

Notebook open, she reads from it, her eyes widening when she gets to the bottom. Me being curious, my Dragon chuckles at my word choice, I look down at the notebook but do not see any words. Carefully, I reach for Luna's hands, but she notices me and moves the paper tablet behind her back. My Dragon laughs, finding this funny.

"Ghost writing isn't meant for mortal eyes, Cairo."

"I'm not mortal."

"Still..." She shakes her head. "I... no."

"Will you at least tell me what it says? I *am* the true sovereign of this realm."

"You won't like it, Cairo," she replies, tucking the notepad in her shirt.

"Luna!"

"He has an army of ghosts, about 50,000, and tonight... they march." My Dragon stills. "I need to talk to Flame." I roll my eyes at the mention of his name, that Angel bastard. "And, I think it's time I have words with my birth father."

For Your Information

Terms You Need To Know

Sups - Supernaturals

Soulie - Necromancers' term for soulmate

Mate - Dragons' term for soulmate

Smooch - Fairies' term for soulmate

The Royals of Faeven

Excellency - Cairo

Dark Fairies' Royalty -
    King Stephen
    Princess Za'Riyah

Light Fairies' Royalty - Queen Victoria

Necromancer Royalty -
> King Alastair
> Queen Lilliana
> Prince Landon
> Prince Leonardo
> Princess Luna

Elf Royalty - King Maximillian

The Six Realms

Earth
The Woodlands
Faeven
Mercury Realm
The Highlands
Galaxy

Ghost 101 Index

Ghost 101: #1—Many people assume your senses disappear when you die, but that's not completely accurate. Ghosts have four of the five senses: sight, smell, sound, and touch.

Ghost 101: #2—It's not uncommon for a ghost to not remember its name. Depending on how long ago they died, they forget who they are, how they died, and other important details about their life. Of course, each ghost is different.

Ghost 101: #3—All ghosts have moments where they relive their deaths. Some relive it in its entirety. Others only relive bits and pieces. It depends on the ghost, and it comes when it wants to come. There's no controlling it.

Ghost 101: #4—After ghosts re-experience their death, they never remember they've relived it. Bringing it up does more harm than good, so it is best to pretend it didn't happen.

Ghost 101: #5—Ghosts gain control over physical objects the longer they've been dead. Newer ghosts—the ones who just passed away—can push buttons or knock things over, but it doesn't happen overnight. It requires practice. Ghosts who've been dead ten or more years can interfere with electricity and manipulate the climate in a particular room. Ghosts who've been dead for thirty-plus years, otherwise known as "the headaches"—I suggest everyone steer clear—can body-jump, meaning they can take over your body and dump you into their ghost one.

Ghost 101: #6—Ghosts can body swap with any living person and Supernatural, I assume, since they are technically alive, except me. I don't know why, but there's something in my blood that prevents them from doing so. Of course, there's a way around this, as there is with almost everything in life. If I grant the ghost my permission to body swap, only then are they able to do so. I was tricked into discovering that.

Ghost 101: #7—Salt is a great medium for keeping ghosts out of your home or entrapping them. However, the older the ghost, the less effective the salt. Now, salt mixed with my blood? No ghost can overpower that.

Ghost 101: #8—There are two options to rid yourself of ghosts. You can release their souls. That means sending their souls to what I call the waiting room, where a reaper will guide them to what's next. Heaven or Hell, that is. I can do this both voluntarily and involuntarily. Voluntary usually means the ghost has accomplished their unfinished business and their spirit is at peace, so they ascend by themselves. Involuntary is me forcing the release, which hurts like hell for them and tires the hell out of me. Sending them back to their places of death is what I did with Riyah earlier. That can also be both voluntary and involuntary as well. Usually, it's always involuntary and not permanent, but it requires less of my energy. It's my go-to.

Ghost 101: #9—Ghosts typically do not like sharing a living or undead body. If multiple ghosts share a body, it means they were all equal in terms of power or have been dead around the same time. If you see a single ghost in one body, he's extremely powerful and has been dead for centuries.

Thank You

Thank you so much for reading
Boo! Can You See Us? Faeven Realm Book One.

If you enjoyed this book,
please leave a review.
Authors love reviews,
and they are greatly appreciated.

Bonus Scene

Need more of Luna and Cairo?

Don't miss your opportunity to read a
FREE *bonus scene!*

Getting your copy is easy!

Like and **follow** Desy
on her social media,
and then send a DM
with your screenshot proof
to receive your exclusive content.

Follow Me

Follow **Desy Smith Author's Page** on Facebook
www.facebook.com/AuthorDesySmith/

Follow **Floebe Publishing** on Instagram
www.instagram.com/floebepublishing/?hl=en

*Don't forget
to dm your screenshot proof
and request your free bonus scene!*

f facebook.com/AuthorDesySmith

ALSO BY DESY SMITH

If you love *Boo! Can You See Us?* check out

my other books

on these platforms:

Amazon

Barnes and Noble

Apple Books

Kobo

Made in the USA
Middletown, DE
19 September 2022

10666503R00055